JANIL SEEGARS

Again

First edition

This book was professionally typeset on Reedsy.
Find out more at reedsy.com

For the ones who believe in second chances.

"Second chances are not given to make things right but to prove we can be better even after a fall."

–Unknown

Contents

Author Note

Please be aware this story involves sensitive topics such as infertility struggles, infidelity, and depression. Although some of these situations are referenced in the work and happen off-page, I still advise you to consider your own health and well-being before diving into Jax and Amina's story.

The Playlist

01./ Let it Be by Dondria
02./ ilym by John K. (feat. ROSIE)
03./ Cry with You by Jeremy Zucker
04./ Every Kind of Way by H.E.R.
05./ Mourning Doves by Jhené Aiko
06./ Seasons by 6LACK (feat. Khalid)
07./ Always Been You by Jessie Murph
08./ I Do by Jessie Reyez
09./ Damage by H.E.R.
10./ First Time by TEEKS
11./ Whenever, Wherever, Whatever by Maxwell

1

Amina

"Don't look back. Don't look back. *Don't. Look. Back.*"

I must look like a madwoman, running through the airport like a bat out of hell with the wheels of my suitcase protesting loudly and all the equipment in my carry-on—my camera, my laptop, an assortment of memory cards, and at least four thousand dollars worth of lenses—bouncing around in their respective slots as I swerve through the crowd. Running—the exercise, not the act of avoiding problems—isn't usually my thing, but I'm trying to lose sight of the one man I was hoping not to see before I managed to pour myself into one of the carefully selected outfits I packed for this trip to Tulum. All of which were chosen for the sole purpose of rendering every man who laid eyes on me speechless.

Every man or just him? My subconscious sneers, her catty words and superior tone making me trip over my own feet. I stumble for a second, narrowly avoiding launching my overpacked suitcase at a young mother pushing a stroller with a sleeping newborn back and forth with her foot, and force myself to slow down before I hurt myself or someone else. And despite the order I gave myself the moment I spotted him hopping out of the back of an Uber Black, I allow myself to look back. To search for the tall and muscular frame, for the once-familiar broad set of shoulders, the rich luster of golden, brown skin I used to study before I fell asleep, the midnight black hair with waves deeper than the ocean. He used to keep it cut low all around, but from the quick glance I got of him—okay it was more than a glance—it's longer now. Surprisingly sexy curls springing from his scalp at the top blending with the waves I spent my teenage years obsessing over at the sides and back. It's a good look on him.

Then again, there isn't much that doesn't look good on Jaxon Daniels. There never was.

When my quick scan of the crowd turns up empty, I breathe a sigh of relief and continue towards my assigned gate. After I check my suitcase, I still have an hour to kill before my flight leaves, so I spend it editing pictures and responding to inquiries because I know once I land Lyric will be on my ass about doing anything that isn't related to her *wedding*. I roll my eyes at the thought. Usually, I love weddings. I mean it's kind of a requirement when you're a wedding photographer and the brains behind The Collective—the most sought-after photography and videography company on the East coast. People falling in love and throwing expensive ass parties to celebrate their connection is my bread and butter, and it's even more heartwarming that my big sister is now one of those people. So it's not the wedding I'm annoyed with, just the person she's getting married to.

Liar. You love Rob.

My mind wanders to the goofy, comic book obsessed research scientist who treats my sister like a queen and would do anything—including spending a week in Mexico before their destination wedding—to put a smile on her face. Yeah, I love Rob, and I love Lyric and Rob together, which can only mean that my annoyance with this entire situation has nothing to do with either of them and everything to do with the fact that I'm taking time off of work during peak wedding season to spend a week at a Cerros resort trying to avoid *him*. Except avoiding him will be impossible because in this grand celebration of love, he's the best man and I'm the maid of honor.

"This is the final boarding call for flight 89B to Tulum. All passengers please proceed to Gate 3 immediately..." The disembodied voice over the PA system startles me out of my reverie. My head snaps up, and I look around, realizing that everyone who was sitting around me has already made their way to the gate. As quickly and carefully as possible, I pack my laptop back into my bag, pull out my boarding pass and ID, and sprint to the gate. The attendant—a short Black lady who looks to be around my mom's age—at the end of the narrow hallway leading to the plane smiles kindly at me as she takes my pass and scans it. I try to smile back, but almost missing the flight because I was agonizing over being around Jaxon has me feeling even more anxious.

"Oh!" She flashes me a bright smile and hands my pass and ID back. "It looks like you've been upgraded to first class."

My brows dip inward. "First class? No, there must be some mistake."

I always fly business class. Even though I can afford to fly first now, I never do. I just never wanted to be one of those people looking and feeling out of place among all the luxury and glamour. There's nothing worse than people taking one look at you and knowing you don't belong there. Knowing that even though your bank account says you're one of them now, it didn't always.

The lady shakes her head and gives me a tight smile. One that reminds me we're short on time, and I have to get my ass on this plane regardless of if there's been a mistake or not.

"If it is a mistake, ma'am. It's certainly a happy one. Enjoy your flight."

"Thanks," I say stiffly, fishing my phone out of my pocket to see if I got any notifications about a change in my flight information, but the only thing there is a text from Lyric.

Lyric: Enjoy your flight, sis. I'll see you soon. :)

Oh. I breathe another sigh of relief and a small smile crosses my lips as I realize that Lyric must have called and upgraded my ticket. She probably was just trying to do something nice before subjecting me to a week of hell. With that thought in my mind, I make my way onto the plane, moving through the open curtains of the economy and businesses class before arriving at first-class where another Black woman—this one younger with smooth brown skin and long ebony tresses—ushers me to my seat and asks me if I would like a glass of champagne. My answer, which was about to be a resounding hell yes, dies on my lips when we arrive at the first row where a familiar form is sitting by the window.

A small gasp breaks free from my lips before I can clamp them shut, which draws his attention from the window to my face, and despite the months I spent preparing for this exact moment, I still feel like my legs have been swept out from under me the moment his gaze touches mine because *it's there*. It's all there. Every second of our history is written on his face. Every kiss, every hug, every contended sigh and moan etched inside rings of smoky quartz and gold.

His lips part and I know whatever he's about to say is going to be just as devastating as what he's doing to me with his eyes. Know it like I know my name. Like I know the story behind every scar on his body. The faint crescent moon on the corner of his mouth from when Rob pushed him face-first into their mom's rose bushes. The jagged patch of slightly darker skin on his forearm from his first attempt at homemade caramel when the syrupy brown liquid bubbled angrily and he got too close. The calluses on his fingers and hands from hours upon hours of practicing his knife work.

"There's nowhere to run, Amina."

Both sides of his mouth quirk, and it takes me a full second to process the fact that he saw me running from him. Saw me going into full track star mode only to end up lowering myself into the seat next to him with his teasing words burning a hole in my brain. My body is stiff as I settle into my seat, and listen to the flight attendants give a full run-down of safety protocols and procedures. Thankfully, there's a ton of space, which makes it easy for me to avoid touching him. The distance doesn't do much to prevent me from inhaling his scent with every breath I pull into my lungs, though. And it doesn't stop me from being painstakingly aware of him glancing at me every now and then, probably wondering when I took a vow of silence, as the plane takes off.

We're in the sky for a full hour before I start to breathe normally and the tension in my shoulders eases a little. Enough for me to reach into my bag and pull out my laptop, hoping to squeeze in a little more work and distract myself from the man sitting beside me. Unfortunately for me, the screen won't come on, nothing but the red battery symbol flashing in obstinate blackness, and no matter how many keys I tap or how many desperate pleas I make to the heavens above, it won't turn on. I have to force myself not to laugh maniacally as I shove it back in my bag and sit back in my seat.

Beside me, Jaxon presses the call button, summoning a flight attendant almost immediately and making me roll my eyes as she saunters over and smiles at him.

"What can I get for you, Mr. Daniels?"

"Two glasses of champagne, please."

His voice is satin-laced gravel, and the smile he gives her makes *my* core clench, so I can only imagine what it's doing to her right now. She manages to look unaffected even as her voice takes on a sultry lilt when she says, "My pleasure, sir."

I make a disgusted sound in the back of my throat as she walks away, and I think I see his shoulders shaking with laughter, but by the time she comes back with a tray with two flutes of champagne—handing one to him and the other to me—they're still again. I hold the glass in my hand, twirling the thin stem between my fingers and wondering why he would think I want anything from him.

"Drink, Amina. It'll help you relax."

Hearing my name on his lips again makes me jolt, and I can't stop my head from swiveling in his direction. He doesn't look the least bit surprised that his order pulled a reaction out of me. I've always been a brat, eager to defy him, to remind him that I might submit to his will eventually, but I'll never do so without a fight.

But I don't have to do it at all anymore.

"I'm not thirsty, Jaxon."

"But you are tense. I can see the knots in your shoulders from here."

I watch his lips curve around the rim of the glass. He lets the pale gold liquid swirl around his mouth, and for the briefest moment, I imagine what it would be like to taste it on his lips. *Shut that shit down, Amina.* I look away from him. "My knots aren't your business." *Haven't been for quite some time.*

"You're right. I guess I'll just have to keep my mouth shut when I see your shoulders swimming around your ears all week."

Warmth starts to spread through my chest, some stupid, unruly part of me being affected by him acknowledging how stressful this week will be for me. I stomp it out before it goes too far.

"That would be for the best."

"God." He laughs. "I almost forgot how fucking stubborn you are."

Almost. Like he tried to let the information slip away but it refused to leave. Refused to be pushed away by time or distance or ugly, unpredictable endings that don't quite fit the beautiful beginnings they grew from.

"Are we going to talk about it?"

This time when I turn to look at him, he is surprised. His dark brows lift, and his pupils expand just a bit. I study him, taking in details with the kind of discernment photographers use when they're scanning a picture for imperfections they can edit out. Except with Jaxon, I don't see any imperfections. *I never have.* All I see is the rigid set of his jaw that's clearly evident under the thick hair of his beard, the proud slope of his nose over a set of lips that would be considered too pouty on most men but somehow work on him.

My mouth goes dry, and I curse myself for being such a brat about the champagne because I can't drink it now even though I really want to. "Talk about what?"

I know exactly what he's talking about. The elephant in the room. The reason why we're here together, in such close quarters after two years of abiding by some unspoken shared custody agreement that kept us from having to give up our favorite places and people when we gave up on each other.

He takes a long sip of his champagne, emptying the glass before turning his gaze back on me. "Your sister marrying my brother."

Even though I try not to, I flinch. The way I always do when I think about Lyric changing her name from Pierce to Daniels, marrying into the family I walked away from.

I shrug. "Why would we need to talk about that?"

"So you can help me figure out what to call Lyric."

"I believe the term is 'sister-in-law,' but I'm sure she wouldn't mind if you just called her by her name. Hell, you can even call her *Mrs. Daniels if you're nasty.*"

I bite the inside of my cheek and flush when Jaxon fixes me with a hard stare instead of laughing at my lame attempt to add some levity to this moment.

6

"I can't do that," he says quietly.

"Why not?"

"Because doing that only makes me think about how everyone should still be calling *you* Mrs. Daniels."

2

Jax

Looking at my wife never gets old. Even after years of catching nothing more than a glimpse of her in a crowded bar in Fairview or the back of her head in pictures Lyric posts on social media, I still find myself in awe of her beauty. The deep, velvet, mahogany of her skin, the copper flecks in her irises that melt into drops of buttered chocolate when her mood changes. The cloud of dark curls that tumble down her back when she frees them from the twisted knot resting on her neck.

I've known her since she was thirteen—back before her body went from straight lines to full, voluptuous curves that are as generous as they are luscious—but she still takes my breath away. And it doesn't matter that we've been divorced for two years or that she hasn't looked at me since I opened my stupid mouth and all but confessed that I still think of her as mine because I'm perfectly content with staring at her, soaking in her beauty and wondering how successful my plan to get her back into my bed and my life will be.

Because that's all I've been able to think about since Rob told me she would be in Tulum the week before the wedding too. He'd sounded scared to tell me, and I guess he should have been because I didn't exactly take it well when he told me about him and Lyric. But in my defense, it was kind of devastating to hear that he fell in love with my ex-sister-in-law while commiserating over the demise of my marriage.

I took this news a lot better though. Mainly because the moment the words settled under my skin, I felt the strongest sense of rightness. Of certainty. Like this week was a gift, a chance to do what I should have done when she asked for the divorce: fight for her.

And now that I know the truth about the end of us, *the entire truth*, and not just the one-sided assumptions and cobbled together memories filled with resentment and hurt, I feel like I have a chance at actually winning.

I thought I'd be the only one flying out today since Lyric and Rob left for Mexico last night and I know Amina hates to travel alone, but by some small miracle, we ended up on the same flight and arrived at the airport within moments of each other. I spotted her first, which gave me the unique opportunity to watch her take off like a bat out of hell when she saw me get out of my Uber. My first instinct was to go after her, but I stopped myself because getting detained for chasing a single woman through the airport is never a good look. Instead, I called my assistant and gave her all of Amina's information, so she could call the airline and upgrade her ticket to first class. Putting her in the extra seat I always purchase when I fly, to avoid having to make small talk with strangers, just so I could have the honor of being ignored by her for the six hours it took for us to reach our destination.

I don't think I've ever been so happy to be ignored by someone, but that's what Amina does to me. She makes everything—even the most mundane or insulting thing—feel like a gift. A rare pleasure you should be down on your knees thanking her for even though you've got nothing from the experience except the chance to share air with her.

And we've been sharing air for hours.

On the plane, in the airport as we picked up our luggage, outside of the airport while we waited for the car Rob sent for us to arrive, in the car on the thirty-minute drive to the Cerros resort where she rolled down the window and pulled in lungfuls of fresh air just to expel me from her body. The only break she's gotten from me is when she escaped to her villa, which happens to be right beside mine, to change for dinner, but now she's back in my orbit. Back to giving me nothing but a prime time view of the twin curves of her ass as she follows the winding path from our villas to the on-site restaurant Lyric and Rob asked us to meet them at. Her sandals slap the bleached concrete with every step, which I'm almost certain she's trying to keep at a reasonable pace because she doesn't want to look like she's running from me. *Again.*

I laugh lightly as the vision of her breaking out into a full sprint flashes through my mind. Warm wind swirls around me, carrying the sound to Amina's ears and whipping the hem of her dress—a backless cream number with a plunging neckline that makes it obvious she doesn't have a bra on—up around her legs when she spins around and glares at me.

"What's so funny, Jaxon?"

For a moment I forget I was laughing. I forget these are the first words she's spoken to me since our brief conversation on the plane. I forget she's no longer mine, and even though she's stopped moving, I keep walking towards her. Only stopping when her round eyes go wide and her entire body tenses like she's bracing for impact.

I stop just in front of her, close enough to see the tiny beauty mark above her left eyebrow. "You running from me for the second time today."

"I'm not running from you."

Another warm breeze blows in, slow and lazy like the strokes of my dick that used to make her squeeze her legs around my hips and moan my name. Her lavender and vanilla scent washes over me, branding me from the inside out. A welcome sensation after years of tepid sexual encounters with women who haven't even come close to lighting the fire Amina's managed to stoke in my veins with just five words.

"Really? Because that's what I call you moving at twice your normal pace instead of walking with me when we're going to the same place."

Her head tilts to the side and tendrils of long curls brush her arm. "Funny. And what word would you use to describe your habit of making everything *I* do about you?"

Obsession. Reckless compulsion. *Love.*

"I'd rather hear which word you'd use."

She blinks, surprised that I'm handing her a chance to insult me. Clearly, she doesn't know I'll take anything she's willing to give me. An insult. A slap to the face. A kick to the balls. As long as she's close enough to deliver the blow.

"Delusion."

My brows lift, and I smile at her, which catches her off guard. "You were always better at choosing words than I was."

"Why do you keep doing that?"

"Doing what?"

"Bringing up the past." I give her a confused look even though I know exactly what she's talking about, and she scoffs. "On the plane, you said 'God, I almost forgot how stubborn you are' and now you're talking about how I always handed you your ass when we would argue."

"I never said that."

"You didn't have to." Her eyes flash, a brilliant explosion of copper and bronze. "We both know it's true. Just like we both know you've used every single interaction we've had today to try and goad me into taking a walk down memory lane with you."

I clench my hands into fists just to keep myself from reaching out and grabbing her, from taking her starlight into my hands and holding it close enough to obliterate me. The idea of any part of us being resigned to the past, deemed an insignificant relic of an era that has been forgotten, makes my entire being ache.

Amina could never be my past.

Our love—our history, our future, and even this impossible present where she won't acknowledge that she's mine— lives in a place where time doesn't exist. A boundless space where the brand she left on my heart has never faded. A ceaseless oasis that will continue to be even when this world is gone and our bodies are nothing but dust floating in the cosmos. This, among other things, is what I'm here to tell her. What I plan on spending this entire week getting her to understand.

"The only place I'm trying to get you to walk with me is to dinner."

My voice is smooth, but my movements are smoother as my hand acts on its own accord and grips her waist, spinning her back around so she's no longer facing me. Amina makes a small sound, it sounds like a mix between a yelp and a gasp, at the contact, which makes letting go of her that much harder. Somehow I manage to do it though, and this time I tuck my hands in the pockets of my pants just to make sure I don't cross her boundaries again.

I chance a glance at Amina and see that she's struggling to hide her body's reaction to my touch, which makes me ridiculously happy. Her nipples have hardened into small tight little buds, that I know are berry brown underneath the wisp of fabric keeping them from me, and her shoulders, along with her spine, have gone stiff. Racked with tension I'm itching to expel with my fingertips.

For a moment, she looks like she's going to say something, but the words never come. Instead, she clears her throat and starts walking again, this time at her normal pace. Her arms brush mine as we navigate the narrow path together, and I think my brain short circuits every time we collide. This is the most I've touched her in years, and I don't know how to process it all. Her scent, her heat, her proximity. The pure perfection of her body moving next to mine makes images of her moving underneath me and on top of me flash in front of my eyes on a loop that doesn't stop until I'm looking at the surprised faces of my brother and future sister-in-law.

"How was the flight?" Lyric asks, pulling Amina into a short hug before coming over to me. She's tall, nearly taller than I am, with the same beautiful mahogany skin as her sister. But where Amina is all soft curves, Lyric is sharp lines. Willowy frame, long legs, piercing eyes, and bright red microlocs that she has piled up on top of her head in a messy bun.

"It was okay."

Amina says at the same time I say, "It was great."

I catch her not-so-subtle eye-roll right before Rob pulls her into a bear hug. His arms wrap around her waist and squeeze tight while she giggles and flails around, trying to force him to release her. This time I'm the one rolling my eyes, an irrational sense of jealousy coursing through my veins because I've spent the better part of the day around her and haven't gotten so much as a smile while Rob flexes one big muscle and she softens immediately.

Perks of not being her ex-husband.

When they're finally done with their little show, Lyric looks as done with them as I am, which makes me feel marginally better. Although, she's probably more embarrassed than annoyed. We all sit down at the table, with Amina and Lyric across from Rob and me, and talk about the wedding and our plans for the week before the conversation shifts to our parents and work.

Amina talks animatedly about her growing business, and I hang on to her every word even though I already know about most of the things she's saying because I make a point of keeping up with her on social media. Watching her photography business grow from a one-woman operation to The Collective—a full-blown team of creatives who work their asses off to make the most important day of people's lives even more special—has been one of my only sources of joy since the divorce. It doesn't stop me from wishing that I would have been by her side while she did it, though.

Conversation continues to flow easily, with Rob talking about some research findings from his latest study at work that no one but Lyric understands because she's the only other nerd at the table. They're in the middle of some weird mind-meld when a pair of servers come out with an array of dishes and drinks, effectively ending their science talk and moving everyone's focus to the food.

"Damn, did you guys order the entire menu?" Amina laughs as she grabs the platter full of plantain chips with a generous serving of shrimp ceviche in the middle. Her eyes are bright and happy, shining in a way I haven't been privy to in a long time.

A sudden twinge of pain runs through me at the sight, and I rub my chest, hoping no one notices how hard I'm staring at her. Then Rob's knee bumps into mine as he shoots me a weird look out of the corner of his eye, and that hope is crushed immediately.

"We were hungry!" Lyric says as she slides a plate full of chicken tacos closer to their side of the table. "And you know how bad I am about making food choices when I'm hungry."

Rob reaches for the plate of tacos, managing to snag one before she swats his hand away. "Yeah, babe. We also know how stingy you get, now hand those tacos over and I'll think about letting you have some of this guacamole."

"Oh, baby. You can keep that guac because these tacos are staying right here with me."

13

"Damn." Amina frowns at her sister. "What about me?"

Lyric waves a hand. "Don't act like we don't see you hogging that ceviche. Poor Jax has been eyeing it since it hit the table."

All eyes swing to me, and I hope the hair of my beard is thick enough to hide the heat rising in my face. Lyric tries to hide her smirk inside the corn tortilla she's lifting to her mouth, but I see it and know immediately that she just wanted to call attention to the fact that I haven't been able to take my eyes off of my wife since she started eating. As a chef, I'll always have a certain appreciation for watching people enjoy food, especially if it's something I've made, but watching Amina eat is like a religious experience.

Like looking into the face of God or having serotonin and dopamine injected straight into your veins and being able to feel every ounce of it flow into your body. Up into your brain until every pleasure center that exists there is dialed up to one hundred times its normal setting. Down into the pit of your stomach, setting off sparks of heat and languid need that refuse to be ignored or denied. That's what seeing her mouth open to allow another morsel of food in does to me. That's what the flash of her tongue, lush and pink, swiping over her lower lip to capture a drop of lime juice that was mad enough to prefer to exist outside the wet heat of her mouth does to me.

Makes me hard. Makes me desperate. *Makes me wish I was a damn plantain chip.*

Everyone is still staring at me, but the only pair of eyes that matter are a wild smattering of copper swimming with thoughts I can't decipher. She's gotten good at hiding from me. Before, I would have written it off as a byproduct of the divorce, but now that I know the real reason she left, a truth I've been sitting with for weeks, I have to accept that she had those skills when we were married too. That they carried her through the divorce she initiated but didn't truly participate in. Most divorces involve some type of mediation, to see if things can be mended or worked out, but Amina wouldn't play ball. She wouldn't see me. She wouldn't take my calls. She sent Lyric to our home to collect the things she left. She didn't even fight for anything. The house. The half of the money I'd made in the last few years of our marriage, which she was legally entitled to. *Nothing.* But I still gave all of it to her anyway.

I hold her gaze and take a sip of the Modelo the server placed in front of me.

"Did you—" Amina shifts in her seat, and I wonder if she can tell what I'm thinking. "Did you want some?"

I shake my head slowly and use my free hand to adjust myself in my pants. "No. I don't want any ceviche, Amina."

Her eyelids flutter like they did on the plane when I said her name, and I smile to myself. She's not as unaffected as she appears to be. *Interesting.*

"Well." Rob clears his throat. "If y'all are done making dinner awkward as hell, Lyric and I have something we want to tell you."

Amina and I both freeze, and it's the first time since I've been back in her presence I don't feel good about our actions being synchronized because I know the place that created that synchronicity—it's a deep, ugly well of pain and heartbreak—and it's not where I want either of our minds to be. But it's the only place we can go right now when a couple that's already engaged, already living together, already done everything worth doing and announcing except procreate, sits you down for dinner and says they have something to tell you. How many times have we sat through this exact same speech? The 'we weren't even trying, it just happened' speech that doesn't make you feel any better about someone else getting what you've always wanted.

The uncomfortable twinge in my chest intensifies, turns into a burning fire that makes me want to stand up, walk around the table and drag Amina away from this conversation. She turns her gaze to her sister, but I'm still looking at her when she says, "What's up?"

Lyric reaches over and grabs Rob's hand. She beams at him then turns to us. "We want to elope."

My shoulders sag with relief just as confusion sets in. "Elope? We're literally here for your wedding."

An event I've spent the last year and half-listening to Lyric gush about anytime I made the mistake of agreeing to come over to her and Rob's house. I know every detail by heart: the name of the flowers in her bouquet, the specific cut and color of the bridesmaid dresses, the exact note the violinist will play when the doors open and Lyric walks down the aisle in her dress. There's no way all of that planning is about to be thrown out the window for some trip to the courthouse.

Not that there's anything wrong with the courthouse. That's where Amina and I got married. We were so fucking young, so obsessed with belonging to each other in every way possible, it didn't matter that she was wearing a dress straight from her closet and the only people there with us were Rob and Lyric.

"Don't worry, Jax." Rob gives Lyric's fingers a light squeeze. "We'll still have the ceremony on Saturday, we'll just already be married."

"We want the first time we say our vows to each other to be in a more intimate setting." Lyric chimes in, lifting a chip overflowing with guacamole to her mouth with her free hand. "It'll be the four of us. Like when you guys got married."

Amina snorts and her eyes flit to mine for just a second. "Because that worked out so well for us."

"I told Lyric that's what you were going to say," Rob mutters.

"And I told you I don't care. All marriages, including the ones that end in the divorce, start the same way, with vows and rings and promises you have every intention to keep. Sometimes it doesn't work out, but it never stops anyone from doing it. Just like y'all not working out doesn't make us any less inclined to want to start our marriage the same way you did: with our best friends by our side."

Lyric looks between me and Amina, daring either of us to defy her logic. I lift my hands in surrender because for some reason I agree with her, which wins me a sharp smile. Amina rolls her eyes and gives a long-suffering sigh. "Whatever you want, sis."

In a move completely at odds with her usually serious personality, Lyric claps her hands together and lets out a girlish squeal before pulling Amina into a sideways hug. And I don't know if she even realizes she's doing it, but as she hugs her sister back, Amina looks at me. And not in a casual, my-eyes-happened-to-meet-yours kind of way, but in the way she used to look at me. Back when we used to have more than history and distance between us. Back when I was her world and she was mine and we could communicate our thoughts without so much as a word passing between us.

But the moment begins and ends so quickly I'm sure I hallucinated it, and I spend the rest of dinner hoping to see it again.

3

Amina

I slipped up. I let the twisted web of emotions Lyric's words about the elopement inspired burrow deep inside of my chest, and in the midst of their invasion, I dropped my guard. Low enough for the soft, mushy part of me that will always exist for Jax—*see I'm even calling him Jax now*—to come out of hiding and fall right into the bottomless pit of my ex-husband's eyes. It's a dangerous place to be. A place full of inside jokes and haunted memories that promise to gleam like diamonds once you wash away the layer of dust covering them with your tears.

Like the tears you cried when he agreed to the divorce without uttering a single word of protest. Almost like he was relieved to be rid of you. I press my fingernails into the palm of my hand, forcing the thought back into the bubbling pit of despair it resides in. I don't have the capacity to deal with it. Not today. Not at any point this week when I'm supposed to be concentrating on being here for Lyric and using whatever energy I'm not putting into playing the gushing maid of honor into keeping Jax at arm's length.

After Lyric and Rob finished giving us a few details for the elopement, which they want to happen tomorrow evening, and I win the argument about documenting the whole thing, we fall back into surprisingly easy conversation. Hours go by with us talking, laughing, and drinking, and it reminds me of all the time we used to spend together, back when Jax and I were the ones happily in love and Lyric and Rob were doing a shit job of hiding the attraction between them.

Now we're all out on the dance floor with Spanish rap spilling out of the speakers and fairy lights wrapped around the wooden beams casting a romantic glow on the tiled patio. We started off dancing together, all of us as a group so it wouldn't be awkward, but eventually Lyric and Rob gravitated towards each other. And now, they've been wrapped in each other's arms, grinding and swaying and kissing in a way that makes it obvious to me they won't be with us long.

Jax has been circling me, watching me dance with other men. His lithe form blending in between the bodies of other drunken patrons, some American like us but others that are clearly locals looking to hook up with tourists, and making it impossible for me to keep track of his movements. By the time I finish dancing with the tall handsome, stranger that's been glued to me for three songs, I've lost sight of him altogether.

"Do you want to get out of here?" The man asks in a thick, melodic accent. I barely hear his question though, I'm too busy trying to locate the one person here I shouldn't be thinking of at all.

"What?" I turn to the guy, finally realizing what he asked. "Oh, no. I'm sorry."

"No need to apologize, *hermosa*." He dips down, presses a soft peck to my cheek. "Thank you for the dance."

Before I can reply, he's gone, moving across the crowded patio with his eyes set on a woman in a red dress with a near-empty margarita in her hand. I shake my head and laugh to myself, resuming my pointless search for my ex-husband for reasons I don't care to explore.

"If I didn't know any better—" The tip of one callused finger slips down my spine, dragging through the light sheen of sweat on my exposed back as Jax's sin-laced voice curls like smoke in my ear. "—I'd say you were looking for me."

Two warm hands, rough and somehow tender, bracket my waist and spin me around until I'm facing him. Shock has me pulling in a deep breath, and I freeze. I haven't been this close to him in years, but my body remembers him.

19

And nerve endings that have been dormant for years come online just because we're close enough to breathe each other in.

A swell of bodies surges around us, pressing us against each other and enclosing us in a bubble of strangers that swallows us whole because we aren't moving. One of them bumps into me, and, instinctively, I place my hands on Jax's shoulders to steady myself. He turns his attention to my fingers on his shirt, smooth brown against white linen, and he looks surprised and then pleased that I'm touching him. I watch his expression transform and will myself to move my hands off of him, but my body refuses to process the order from my brain.

"I wasn't." His eyes call me a liar, but his mouth stays closed, which makes me want to double down. "I *wasn't* looking for you."

"Then you were keeping track of me." Amusement flickers in the smoky rings of his eyes, and it grows brighter when I can't find the words to deny his assertion. "Tell me why you were keeping track of me, Amina."

The first and only rule I've had for myself after the divorce was to stay far away from Jax. To avoid any situation where he might take the opportunity to use this voice—deep and gravelly with just the right amount of desperation—and those eyes—rich and smoky with every second of our shared history playing on repeat under a fan of unfairly long lashes—to bend my will to meet his needs. I used to love to bend for him. To yield to him. To let him use me for his needs because I could always trust him to meet mine.

Fuck, don't think about that now.

"Because I wanted to see you coming."

His fingers flex against my back, sending sparks of desire skating across my skin. "You knew I would come for you."

"I knew you would ignore my requests to be left alone."

"Requests? I haven't heard you make any requests. If I had, I would have honored them."

I scoff, and the sudden motion makes my nipples brush against his chest. "No, you wouldn't have."

"Yes, I would. Tell me what you want, Amina. I'll give you anything. It's all yours anyway."

"Pretty sure that stopped being the case when we signed the divorce papers."

His hand slides lower, and the tip of his pinky grazes the low cut lace hugging my hips as he studies me. Whiskey eyes taking in all of my features and stealing my breath.

"I don't give a fuck about those papers. Everything I have is yours, and it always will be because I wouldn't have any of it if it wasn't for you."

I close my eyes for a brief second, shielding myself against the conviction in his tone and the soul-crushing truth shining in his eyes. Jax has always been a passionate man. I've always known it, always loved it about him, but right now, I hate it. I hate the way he can go from death-like calmness to having tidal waves of heat and devastation pouring off of him and spiking my pulse.

When I open them again, my throat is tight. Irritation, at him and me, wrapping its fingers around my windpipe and squeezing until red clouds my vision. *Why would he say something like that?* I push against him, forcing him to let me go, and he does so reluctantly.

"Shut up."

His brows knit together. "Shut up?"

"Yes. Shut up. You can't say shit like that to me."

He takes a step towards me, hands flexing like he wants to put them back on me. "Why not?"

"Because you can't! We're not together anymore, Jax, and I don't care if you still think of me as Mrs. Daniels or say that everything you have is somehow mine, which sounds absolutely crazy by the way, we've been divorced for years."

"What if I said that was a mistake?"

Those invisible fingers squeeze harder, making me speak through clenched teeth. "Then I'd tell you to shut up again."

"But you wouldn't tell me I'm wrong."

"Jax—"

"There you guys are!" Lyric's voice snaps me out of the trance Jax has me in, and I spin around quickly to face her. The crowd has thinned a bit, and the small group around us parts as soon as they see Rob coming. "We've been looking for you everywhere."

She glances between us, her eyes somewhat glossy from alcohol and happiness, and I can tell she knows something has happened between us.

Has something happened between us?

"We're heading back to our room," Rob says, wrapping one arm around my sister's waist. "Lyric is tired. Are you guys going to be okay?"

I feel Jax moving in closer, the heat of his skin pouring into my back, and I step up to keep my ass from brushing against any part of his body.

"Actually, I think I'll head back with you guys. I wanted to run a few things by you guys for tomorrow."

Lyric and Rob look at each other, and it's evident to me that the last thing they want is company on their way back to their room. Any other time, I'd take the hint and leave them to it, but I have to get away from Jax.

Before either of them can answer, I loop my arm through Lyric's and start walking off of the dance floor. She doesn't say a word as we head out, with Rob and Jax on our heels, but I can feel her curious looks on the side of my face every so often.

Our walk back is quiet and quick. When we reach the stretch of beachfront villas that Jax and I are staying in, Lyric and Rob say goodnight and practically skip off, leaving me and Jax alone in front of my room.

His hands are in his pockets, his eyes on me, and it takes everything in me to turn on my heel and start moving towards my door. My fingers are shaky as I press the key card against the electronic padlock, and just as the light turns from red to green, I feel him.

His breath is warm, warmer than the late-night air, as he runs his nose along my shoulder and up my neck, making sure his lips touch every goosebump the motion creates.

"Turn around."

Something inside of me—the last shred of my sanity, perhaps—snaps in two. Every bit of my ability to resist him at this moment slips out of my grip as I turn to face him. He looks pleased, *infinitely so*, and it makes me feel like there's nothing I won't do to keep that expression on his face.

Pull it together, girl.

I wish I could, but Jax isn't giving me any time or space to process anything that isn't him. His eyes burn into mine as he leans forward, his lips making a beeline for my mouth then bypassing it all together to land on my collarbone.

"Jax—" I try to sound upset, but even I recognize there's no conviction in my tone. That my hands are at my sides, hanging limply, instead of on any part of his body pushing him away, stopping him from making lazy circles with his tongue at the base of my neck and hiking one of my legs up until it's wrapped around his hip.

I want to stop him. I truly do, but the years I've spent dreaming of his lips on my skin pale in comparison to the real thing. I feel like I've just had a syringe full of adrenaline plunged into my heart and emptied in an instant. Under his touch, I'm alive and vibrant in a way that I haven't been since the last time we were together, just a week before the opening of his restaurant, Arcane.

We were so good that day, better than we had been in months. Because between Cassidy Marks—his biggest investor—monopolizing his time, dragging him to meetings and events all under the guise of making connections that would ensure the success of the restaurant, and the stress of undergoing consistently unsuccessful fertility treatments, it felt like we were always being pulled in different directions.

But that day, Jax came home early from work. We cooked dinner together. We made love on the couch and cuddled and talked like we used to when we were teenagers who wanted nothing more than to spend hours listening to the other person's voice. And then Jax said he didn't want to keep doing IVF, and all hell broke loose.

I felt like he had pulled the rug out from under me. Like he went back on every promise he'd ever made me. Like he looked at our life, at our struggles and my failure, and decided it wasn't worth the trouble. Like he changed his dream, and I was the last one to find out about it. That argument had so many painful layers to it, sharp twists and turns that took us from a conversation about his concern for my well being to me hurling ugly, hurtful words at him, accusing him of sacrificing our dreams of having a family to make more time for his new life, full of lavish dinners, high-class people and *Cassidy*.

And right when we were in the thick of it, she called.

It wasn't the first time one of her 'urgent calls' cut into our time together, she was always calling with some important update or outlandish idea, but it was the first time I wholly expected Jax to let it go to voicemail. To put us in front of her and the restaurant, but he didn't. He just let out a long, tired sigh, told me he was sorry, and asked me to wait while he sorted this out real quick. I don't know how long it actually took for him to wrap up the conversation, though, because as soon as he walked out of the room to take the call in private, I left. And I stayed gone for days, sleeping in Lyric's guest room and dodging his calls and pleas to see me, until the night of the opening. When I showed up to the restaurant early, hoping to reconcile, and got slapped in the face with the ugliest reality.

The heartbreaking memory floods my brain, its jagged edges brushing against the desire brewing there, threatening to slice it in half. But then Jax's fingers are trailing up my leg, blazing a fiery path from the ankle pressed against his back, to the knee bent at his hip and up, up, up until he's palming one of my ass cheeks. The tips of his long fingers just barely grazing the lips of my sex, which is throbbing against his erection through the barriers of my lace boy shorts and his pants.

"I miss you," he breathes. "Do you ever miss me, Mina? Do you ever think about me and regret every second we've spent apart?"

He chooses that exact moment to come up for air. His lips leaving my neck, so he can look at my stunned face. And I almost wish he would have stayed where he was because the moment our gazes lock I'm reminded of the promises he made while he stared into the depths of my soul and claimed every inch of it for himself, and I can't help but wonder how many women he's looked at that way. How many women he's given those forever eyes to. *How many times he gave them to her.*

At one point in my life, I never would have believed he would give them to anyone but me. But that was before Little Miss Wide Eyes and Deep Pockets walked into his life and served him his dreams on a silver platter with her panties as a complementary side. Picturing them together—the muscles in Jax's back strained and damp with sweat as he works his length into her, feeding her pleasure with every inch, her desperate whimpering in his ear—makes my stomach churn. The images burn like acid and bring me back to my senses.

"No." My voice wavers. I swallow past the lump in my throat and try again, dropping my leg from his grip for good measure. "No, Jax, I don't miss you. I don't think about you, and the only thing I regret is not making it clear to you on the plane that this can't happen."

I finally manage to get my hands working and begin the hard work of peeling his fingers off of me. Losing the heat of his touch doesn't bring me as much relief as I thought it would, but I don't allow myself to stop. Not until the brief connection is severed completely. *Just like the rest of us.* Jax stares at me, his eyes roving over my body, touching all the parts of me that belie my words—my hardened nipples, my pounding heart, my flushed skin—and calling me a liar once again. Only this time his lips part to follow suit.

"You're a bad liar, Amina."

"*Fuck you, Jax.*"

His lips curve into a slow, devilish grin that sends sparks of heat through my core. And I'm so distracted by the sensation, I don't notice Jax closing the small distance between us until he's right on me. His scent—that unique mix of sandalwood and something inherently male and *him*—enveloping me. I press my back to the door, wishing it didn't make me feel completely at home.

Jax rests his forehead against mine, and the entire world shrinks until it consists of nothing but the soft brush of his lips against mine and the warmth of his breath rushing over my skin as he places one of his hands on the door handle behind me.

"I thought you'd take a little bit more convincing." With his free hand, he takes hold of my left one and laces his fingers through mine. He sighs softly and pulls our linked hands to his mouth, pressing a kiss to the knuckle of my ring finger. "But if this is you making a request, you have to know I'll be more than happy to fulfill it."

I suck in a sharp breath. My body once again betraying my words as I melt between him and the door. "It wasn't a request."

"It's not too late for it to become one. Invite me in." Jax whispers, and I can feel his fingers curling around the handle of the door, preparing for the possibility of my yes. "Let me remind you how good we are together."

"I don't want a reminder."

I don't need one. I carry the truth of us with me, curled in a tight ball that rests underneath my breastbone right where my heart used to be.

"Then you need to tell me to leave."

Underneath the strained order is a longing that calls to the part of me that's belonged to him since I was old enough to acknowledge its existence, and I have to squeeze my thighs together to stop the reaction it stirs in me.

My body is waging a war with my mind, and I honestly don't know which one I want to win. *Liar.* Jax's lips ghost over mine, and I know he's trying not to kiss me. He doesn't want to take anything I don't want to give. And no matter what my body is saying, I can't give him this.

"Leave, Jax."

He moves fast, releasing his hold on me and the door handle like one, or both, of us has burned him. And I feel like I've been robbed. Of his heat. Of his proximity. Of his attention. The desperate urge to reclaim all of it swells in my chest, threatening to break through the wall I built to try and contain it. I spin on my heel, fumbling with the key card to unlock the door again. I'm acutely aware of Jax at my back. I half expect to hear him protest, to try and convince me to let him in, but the only thing I hear is his laugh.

A dark, nearly silent, chuckle that caresses my back as I open the door. Just before I step over the threshold I hear him say, "Goodnight, Mina."

4

Jax

The taste of Amina's skin is still on my lips. Or at least the ghost of it is. In reality, I probably washed it away when I brushed my teeth this morning, and if that didn't do it the espresso I'm currently sipping as I listen to my assistant, Grayson Hart, update me on the progress we're making on the location search for the restaurant I want to open in New Haven—a city a little less than an hour away from Fairview—definitely did.

"My favorite is the one downtown. It's closest to the boutique hotel that just opened."

I nod. I'm only half-listening, but I agree with her. "Yeah, I like that one too. Let's have the realtor focus on it specifically."

"I'll call him as soon as we hang up."

"Do you have anything else for me?" I'm anxious to end the call, to get back to Amina. She told me to leave last night, which I fully expected. What I didn't expect were the moments before she sent me away. The way she melted under my touch. The way she let me touch her, kiss her neck, pull in the sweetest, most satisfying, sips of her skin and replace my every breath with her scent.

"Uh—" Grayson hesitates, her eyes flashing nervously between the screen and what I know must be the last item on her agenda. "Ms. Marks called."

My gut twists at the mention of Cassidy Marks, the self-proclaimed Midas of Fairview who makes a habit out of taking her family's money and using it to make a star out of whatever poor bastard she plucked out of obscurity that week. I remember when she found me. I was killing myself, working for an executive chef who was content to take my recipes and slap his name on them to keep his Michelin star and building my own following on social media with pictures Amina took of the meals I'd make in our tiny ass kitchen.

We were so broke back then, refusing to take any money from our parents, desperate to prove ourselves as entrepreneurs in families full of people who swore by the security of college degrees and traditional nine-to-fives. When Cassidy came into our lives, with her money and connections and unwavering belief in what my brand could be, it was a welcome relief. She got me out of that hell hole of a kitchen with my sanity and all of my recipes. And within two years of knowing her, I was making more money than I ever had, opening Arcane—my first restaurant and the cornerstone of my brand—and losing my wife.

Technically, the last one wasn't all Cassidy's doing. That's true. Amina and I fell apart on our own. The stress of trying to start a family while balancing the demands of our businesses made us vulnerable, put us in a place where we couldn't reach each other. But my relationship with Cassidy didn't help. We got too close. *I* let her too close, and I did a shit job of setting boundaries, allowing her to use a professional relationship to cross personal lines because I was so grateful to her for giving me opportunities I could have never secured on my own.

That gratitude turned into something I thought was friendship, and I would feel stupid about believing that except people like Cassidy do a really good job of making you feel like they care about you. They put your names in rooms you won't ever step foot in. They champion your dreams and listen to your fears. They slowly acclimate you to a new reality where their money can get them anything, including unlimited access to you.

And I let it happen.

I listened to her opinion on everything. I changed recipes based on her opinions about what our 'target demographic' would want. I took her calls no matter what. I dropped what I was doing to attend events with her. I shared meals with her and her friends and spent more time in her world than my own.

And when I started to notice the toll trying to conceive was taking on Amina, I leaned on her. I talked to her about things I should have been discussing with my wife. I believed her willingness to listen was innocent, but it wasn't and now I know that confiding in her cost me everything.

Grayson clears her throat, and I realize I haven't responded yet. "What did she want?"

"To discuss the proposal." Another awkward flash between the screen and her notebook where the notes from her call with Cassidy must live. There must be a lot of them. That's what happens when you try to buy your largest investor out. My lawyer, Sean Loewe, told me to expect her to fight back, and I did. I just didn't know the fight would start less than twenty-four hours after he sent the paperwork over. "I told her all communication needed to go through Mr. Loewe, but she wanted to speak to you directly. I told her you were out of the country."

"Thanks, Grayson. Feel free to forward any other calls from her directly to Sean and make sure to take advantage of your tyrant of a boss being out of town this week. Leave early every day this week, come in late, go to the spa, catch up on sleep. Do something for yourself, *please*. You've been doing such great work, and I don't want you to get burnt out. Promise you'll take some time for yourself and spend that bonus money."

She flushes, and I laugh because it's how she always reacts when I tell her how amazing she is at her job. It's not a lie or some outlandish flattery bosses use to make you feel appreciated in every way except your paycheck. Grayson is amazing at her job, and I wouldn't be able to keep a handle on all of the inner workings of the multi-faceted madness that is my brand without her. I gave her a bonus before I left for Tulum for all of the hard work she's put into working with the realtor on the search for the new location and for always keeping my head on straight.

"I promise I'll take a few days off after I get confirmation from the realtor that we've put in an offer on the place we want."

"Then I'll let you go right now, so you can get the ball rolling. Have a good week, okay?"

"I will, and I hope you do too!"

The call ends, and I breathe a sigh of relief as I put my computer away. With that meeting out of the way, I'm free for the rest of the week. Free to pursue my wife. Free to do everything in my power to ensure her brain catches up with her body, which already knows it wants me back.

Pushing to my feet, I slide my room key and phone into my back pocket and abandon the relative cool of my villa for the heat of the scorching sun. It's only eleven in the morning, but I can tell it's going to be humid and hot all day. Even still, there's no denying how beautiful this location is. The Cerros resort is strategically placed, nestled between the beach and the town with bike paths and hiking trails that lead to Mayan ruins.

I can see why Rob and Lyric wanted to get married here. It's absolutely stunning, and I'm not just talking about the white sand beaches and turquoise waters. There's a certain magic and history to this slice of paradise that makes you feel like anything is possible. Like even the most fragile, broken thing can be made whole here. I want that for me and Amina, for us to be whole again. For us to have a million more moments like last night except they don't end with her asking me to walk away from her.

My phone vibrates in my pocket, and I pull it out to see a text from Rob saying him, Lyric, and Amina are at the pool in one of the private cabanas. Immediately, my brain conjures the thought of Amina in a swimsuit. Her curves spilling out of tiny swaths of fabric that get to touch her when I can't, attracting the attention of men she might not send away if they show interest. *Who the hell am I kidding? She's a fucking goddess. Of course, they'll show interest.*

The thought settles under my skin, making it prickle uncomfortably as I maneuver the path towards the only pool on-site with private cabanas. It's near the side of the resort that Rob and Lyric are staying on. While Amina and I both chose beach views, they opted for the jungle rooms—glass structures that are nestled into an array of local plants and trees. All strategically designed to make you feel like you're in the wildest most exotic part of the jungle instead of a guest at a five-star resort.

When I finally make it to the cabana, I stop short. Lyric and Amina are lounging inside, stretched out side by side on the plush white bed in the middle of the wooden structure with white sheets billowing on every side for privacy, but Rob is nowhere to be seen. Not that I would have wasted a second looking at him anyway. No, my eyes are only for Amina. For every exposed inch of velvet skin glistening with the finest sheen of sweat, or water, and inviting me to lap up every drop of it with my tongue. I've been deprived of her, of her body, for years—depending on nothing but my memory of her curves to get me through—and now that I'm standing here, confronted by every inch of her that isn't covered by the canary yellow bikini she's wearing, all I can do is stare.

Honestly, calling it a bikini is pushing it. It's more like a poorly constructed joining of string and triangles. One covering each of her nipples, leaving the lush skin of the rest of her breasts to spill out of the sides and bottom of the cups. There's another sparse triangle at the apex of her thighs, and because her legs are up, both of her heels pressing into the mattress, I can see that calling the thing hugging her ass—the same ass I had the honor of palming just last night—a covering would be generous. Too fucking generous because it's not covering her ass at all. It's just there, surrendering to the demands of skin it's supposed to be in charge of.

And don't get me started on the strings. The strings that loop over her shoulders and kiss her ribs before disappearing around her back to secure the triangles. The strings that sink into the dips at her hips and hide underneath the swell of her belly. The strings that touch her in every place I want to touch her, that are tied in neat little bows making her look like a scarcely wrapped present just for me.

"You okay, Jax?" This from Lyric, who's been watching me stare at her sister with the most devious look in her eye. "You look like you've gotten a bit overheated."

It pains me to drag my gaze away from Amina, who hasn't even acknowledged my presence, and I don't even try to hide that I was staring because I've already been caught.

"Yeah, I'm good. Where's Rob?"

"He went to grab us some drinks." Lyric stands and moves towards the entrance where I'm hovering, frozen. "I'm going to see what's taking him so long."

A surge of gratefulness goes through me as she brushes past me and saunters off towards the pool bar. I don't know why, but it feels like she's trying to help me. With nothing else to focus on, I turn my attention back to Amina. She's still lounging on her back, and her hair is piled up on her head but there are a few loose tendrils framing her face.

"Is this the part where you pounce on me and demand I take you back to my room?"

A long, silent second passes before she opens her eyes and looks at me. When she realizes I haven't come into the cabana even further, haven't so much as taken a step towards her, I swear I see a hint of disappointment flicker in her eyes, but it's gone before I can be certain of it.

"No," I say, keeping my tone cool even though I feel like someone has set my very soul on fire and spelled her name with the accelerant. "Unless you're making a request. If that's the case, I'd be happy to oblige."

She pushes up on her elbows and rolls her eyes. "You wish."

"Yeah, I do."

"Jax."

My heart starts pounding in my chest just from hearing her call me something other than my full name. I haven't heard her call me that outside of the voicemails and videos I kept from our life together in years, and it makes me want to drag her into my arms and kiss her pouty lips. Instead, I drop down onto the patio sofa on the far wall of the cabana facing the bed.

"Mina."

"I need you to stop this."

"I'm not doing anything."

"Yes, you are." I watch her sit up all the way. The movement makes her breasts jostle around, and my dick twitches when part of one berry-brown nipple peeks out, teasing me. "And you've been doing it since yesterday on the plane. It needs to stop *now*."

"Why?"

"Because we're here for Lyric and Rob, not whatever this game is you're playing."

I press my lips together to hold in the laugh crawling up my throat. She thinks this is a game, but I've never been more serious in my life. "I can think of a few games I'd like to play with you, baby, but this—" I gesture between the two of us, and she narrows her eyes. "—is not a game to me. You have never been a game to me. Not even when I was a thirteen-year-old boy obsessed with beating you at everything."

Her expression softens marginally. It's a small relaxing of several muscles, including the ones in her furrowed brows, that only lasts for a few seconds before they harden even more. She lets out a long sigh and swings her legs over the edge of the bed to stand. Her eyes are on the opening of the cabana, and I know she's going to walk out. A sharp twinge of panic flares in my gut, making me want to get on my feet and stop her, but I don't. Nothing but the knowledge that she's not mine, that touching her, let alone stopping her, isn't my right anymore, keeps me glued to my seat.

I'm prepared to let her leave, but then she makes a point of stopping in front of me. Close enough for me to catch her scent. Close enough for me to reach out and grab her hand. Close enough for me to unravel the loose knot on her hip holding her flimsy bathing suit in place. My fingers tingle with the thought of touching her, but I trade my desire to do so for the gift of drinking in her fury.

"We're divorced." Her voice is barely a whisper, but there's heat there. Enough to rival the sun that's high in the sky, scorching everything in its path. "The day we signed those papers, everything else stopped mattering, so *stop* bringing it up."

"No."

"*No?*"

I nod, letting her know she heard me correctly. "No. I won't stop bringing it up. I won't stop thinking about it. Actually, that's wrong, I *can't* stop thinking about it. About you. About us. Signing those papers was the biggest mistake of my life, and I'm going to do everything in my power to make it right."

"That's just the thing, Jax, you can't make it right. We were broken, *ruined*, and we did the only thing you can do when something is shattered beyond repair: we walked away. There is no making it right."

Before either of us realizes what's happening, I reach for her, grabbing her

33

wrist and pulling her forward until she's falling onto the couch beside me. She gives a surprised yelp as she lands on her ass, and I push her down onto her back, following the surrender of her soft curves with a desperate growl. She blinks up at me, processing the fact that I'm on top of her with my weight nestled between her open legs.

Amina's chest rises and falls rapidly, signaling her agitation, but to my surprise, she doesn't try to push me off of her. That makes me feel confident about my next move, which is pinning her arm up over her head and lacing our fingers together while I brush my lips over hers.

"You make the end of our marriage sound so simple, so easy, like letting you go didn't kill me. Like not knowing why I had to figure out how to live life without you hasn't made every fucking day unbearable."

I can feel the heat of her core through the thin fabric of my shorts, and I have no control over my dick swelling in response. Amina's eyes stretch, and she looks shocked but also pleased at my response. That doesn't stop her jaw from turning rigid though.

"You got by just fine, and I'm sure you had plenty of *friends* who were willing to help you with the transition."

The vehemence in her words cuts me, but it's her eyes that destroy me. Reminding me of the day we argued about whether doing another round of IVF was a good idea. It had been a few months since our second round, and I'd promised her we would do three, but the idea of watching her go through the devastation of another failed cycle was too much for me to bear. In my head, it all sounded right, but when it came out of my mouth, it was all wrong. That's when she looked at me like this. With nothing but hurt swimming with the tears in her eyes while she accused me of wanting the glamour of the world Cassidy had inducted me into more than I wanted a family with her.

That was a lie. I never wanted anything more than I wanted her belly round and full, swollen from growing our child.

"Maybe I just got good at living with the pain. Maybe I *had* to be good at living with it because there's nothing in this world—no woman, no amount of money, or fucking drug—that could make me forget your absence for even a second."

34

"Jax." She turns her head to the side, freeing herself from my earnest expression. "Please stop."

Aching from the loss of her lips, I bury my face in her neck. Pressing my lips to her skin and tasting the salt from her sweat. Once again, she surprises me by not pushing me away, so I kiss her again.

"I can't, baby." Her pulse pounds beneath my lips, and I feel mine racing to match it. "I need you."

"No, you don't."

I make a rough, broken sound in the back of my throat, and she shivers against me as I kiss a path from her neck to her collarbone, down to the valley between her breasts.

"I haven't breathed since you left me, Amina."

Logically, I know the statement makes no sense, but it feels like the truest thing I've ever said. Like the only truth that's ever mattered. Because she has to know that despite everything—the restaurants, the homes, the padded bank account, and notoriety—my life isn't worth living without her.

"Don't say that. I can't hear you say that."

There's a tremor in her voice, but I can't tell if it's because she's feeling emotional or because I'm slowly peeling the scrap of fabric hiding her nipple from me away from her breast with my teeth. When I finally manage to work the little triangle all the way to the side, I hear her sigh. Like it's a relief to have even the smallest part of her body bared to me.

"Then I won't say anything else." My breath skates over her skin, and her back bows as I open my mouth further, preparing to suck the tight bud into the heat of my mouth. "I can think of better things to do with my mouth anyway."

I'm lost in the taste of her, but I don't miss the way her back arches off of the couch when I latch onto her. I don't miss the sharp hiss on her lips or the way her thighs tense around my hips, holding me in place, while I lave at her breast. And I damn sure don't miss the way her hand comes up, cupping the back of my head, pressing me into her lusciousness so I can devour her more thoroughly.

"*Jax.*" The whimper falls from her lips, accompanied by the restless churning of her hips against my dick. I grind against her, matching every frenzied swirl with one of my own. "Oh God, what are you doing to me?"

There's no answer to her question that wouldn't shatter this moment, so I don't give her one. Instead, I free her other nipple from the cloth and lavish it with the same attention I gave the first one. Long, decadent pulls on perfect flesh followed by pointed flicks of my tongue that make her legs jerk against me with every stroke. Her reaction makes my heart soar. Because whatever else we may have lost, we didn't lose *this*—the rightness that can only come from me worshiping her body with mine. For some people, it might not mean much, but for me, for right now, it feels like everything.

In some distant part of my brain, I recognize that I should probably pull back because Lyric, Rob, or any one of the guests milling around the pool just a few steps away could walk in and see us like this, but I can't do it. Touching her, tasting her, takes precedence over everything, and I won't be able to stop until I hear her moaning my name while pleasure replaces the blood in her veins.

Amina thrashes underneath me, and when I look up at her, she's staring down at me. Hunger burning bright in her eyes while desire overtakes every one of her features. Her teeth dig into the plump flesh of her lower lip, and for a moment I consider abandoning her breasts to kiss her. She reads my intention clearly and with nothing more than a small shake of her head, denies me the right to her mouth.

A short burst of frustration blooms in my chest, but it dissipates just as quickly as it appeared when her hips start to move with more precision. Like she's finally found the angle she needs to use me for her pleasure. I release her nipple and lift up a bit, so I can watch the show and what I see leaves me breathless. Her bikini bottoms have shifted some, leaving her sex partially exposed and making it possible for me to feel her slick heat through the thin fabric sheathing my erection.

"Fuck, *Mina...*"

Her eyes glow, transforming into those pools of buttered chocolate I want to drown in, before she squeezes them shut and shakes her head. "Shut up. *Shut up.* Don't ruin this with your stupid mouth."

If I wasn't so damn determined to see her unravel underneath me, I'd laugh.

JAX

As it stands, I know she's right because the words crowding my tongue would ruin this moment for both of us. Dazed as I am, I might fuck around and ask her to marry me, which would all but guarantee her never letting me have this, *or more*, again.

And God knows I want more. I want everything.

So I cover her body with mine again, and I suck one breast into my mouth while I work at the other with my hand. Taking one painfully tight nipple between my thumb and forefinger and rolling and pinching and pulling while my tongue flutters over its counterpart relentlessly, and my dick throbs incessantly for the pussy sliding against it, teasing it with the promise of heated ecstasy it might not get to have. I don't know how much time goes by before Amina's back bows, and her eyes squeeze together tighter like she's trying not to look at me, while her orgasm creates a little puddle on the front of my shorts.

I rain kisses all over her skin and continue to grind against her long after she's lost herself in her release just to draw out her pleasure. She whimpers and curses softly under her breath, but I can't help but notice that the one thing I wanted to hear her say in her ecstasy-soaked voice never leaves her lips: my name. It's a blow to my ego for sure, but one I think she meant to deliver. It's an act of defiance, a reminder that she doesn't belong to me and neither does her pleasure, and I would be hurt by it if it didn't turn me on so fucking much.

Her fighting so hard to remind me of the figurative distance between us makes me think she's more worried than she's let on about what the lack of actual distance is doing to her resolve.

And she should be worried because I'm not leaving Tulum without her heart.

37

5

Amina

"Are you sure you're okay?" Lyric asks for the fifth time since I walked into her villa a few hours ago with two spa employees and a waiter pushing a room service cart with enough food and champagne on it to feed an entire bridal party following behind me. Now it's just me and her, lounging around in fluffy white robes and wasting time until we have to get dressed for the ceremony, which Rob has planned all on his own.

He hasn't even given Lyric the full details. All he told her was to show up ready and willing to commit to forever and a day with him. Under normal circumstances, I would fully appreciate how incredibly romantic the gesture is, but the circumstances of this day are anything but normal, especially given what happened between me and Jax in the cabana.

And let's not mention how nerve-wracking it is for a photographer to walk into a shoot blind. All I know is we'll be leaving the resort about an hour before the sun bathes the world in the flawless, golden light that makes everything look a million times more beautiful. I can only hope we'll have reached our destination before that happens, so I can capture the ceremony perfectly.

Anxiety swirls in my gut as I think about it, and I know it's not just because I can't come up with a full game plan for the most important wedding I've ever shot. I mean that's part of it, but the other part is knowing that in a few hours I'll watch my sister promise her life to the man she loves while I'm standing across from my estranged husband who feels decidedly less estranged now.

Now that you let him dry hump you like a teenager, you mean.

The thought slams into my skull and jolts my entire body, causing me to spill champagne from the glass I've been nursing since Lyric popped the bottle onto my robe.

"Shit." I grab a napkin off the table beside me and try to dry it up, but it's no use. "Fuck."

Lyric looks even more concerned as she stares at me. "What the fuck, Mina? Are you—"

"Don't ask me if I'm okay again, Lyric." I laugh mirthlessly and set the flute on the table between us. "You already know I'm not."

"I do. I was just waiting on you to stop wasting your breath lying to me."

"I wasn't trying to lie to you," I mumble, crossing my arms over my chest. "I just wasn't ready to admit the truth to myself."

She twists her lips to the side, trying to hide a smile that tells me she already knows the answer to the question she's about to ask. "Which is?"

"That I should never be left alone in a room with Jaxon Daniels again."

"I KNEW IT! I fucking knew it." Her voice has gone up an entire octave, but I still catch the smug certainty coating her words as she shifts in her seat to face me. "Something happened in the cabana didn't it? I told Rob we needed to take our time bringing the drinks back. There was just something about the way Jax looked at you....like he wanted to eat you alive." She shivers solely for dramatic effect. "When Rob looks at me like that I know exactly what time it is."

"Eww, Lyric." I could have gone my whole life without knowing Jax and Rob, who already look too much alike for their own good, have similar 'come here, so I can devour you" looks. "Please don't ever mention what Rob looks like when he's trying to get you into bed to me again."

She picks up a napkin, wads it up, and launches it at my face. "Oh, grow up, Amina."

"Says the woman behaving like one of the two-year-olds she treats."

"When's the last time you been around a two-year-old? Throwing a napkin is tame compared to how those little monsters act when they come into my office. Especially if they need to get a shot..."

She trails off mid-sentence when she sees my expression has changed. The faintest spark of sadness nibbles at my already raw heart because of her off-hand question. I know she didn't mean anything by it, just like I know I was the one who brought up the kids she sees as a pediatrician, but for some reason, it still hurts. Probably because we both know that even though I love kids, and put myself through hell trying to bring one into the world, I don't spend a lot of time around them because no one in my inner circle has any. She's my only sister, and we're both childless. All of my friends who started families of their own disappeared into mommy groups and play dates, and I let them go because it hurt too much to hold on to them. To watch them have everything I wanted for myself.

Somehow I managed to convince myself I was doing the right thing, that separating myself from painful situations was okay, but in reality, all I was doing was isolating myself. Leaning into my pain when I should have been finding healthy ways to deal with the changes to my life plan. Checking out when I should have been paying attention to the fact that my personal failures were pushing my husband towards another woman. Lyric's hand gripping mine pulls me out of my reverie, and I squeeze her fingers tight, thankful for the rescue even though I can already see the apology on her lips.

"Don't." I give her a small smile. "I'm fine. If anything, your horror stories from work make me rethink the whole kids thing altogether."

It's a lie, and we both know it. Ever since we were kids, Lyric knew she wanted to be a doctor, and all I wanted to be was a mom. And even after all the heartbreak of trying to conceive when Jax and I were married, I still want it.

"It's going to happen for you, Mina, and when it does, you're going to be amazing."

Tears well in my eyes, and I swipe them away as they fall. "Thanks, Lyr."

"You're welcome. Now, tell me the truth. Did you fuck Jax in that cabana?"

* * *

We're on a yacht. My sister is getting married on a fucking yacht, and the only person here who knows how much I hate boats besides me is the one man I promised myself I wouldn't so much as glance at this evening.

It's a good thing I'm not looking at him too. Because if I was I might have noticed the way the sleeves of his cream shirt are rolled past his elbow, showing off every cord in his annoyingly defined forearms, or given myself a reason to obsess over the bulge in his pants and the way it felt nestled against my core when I was stupid enough to let him get me underneath him.

Yes, it's a very good thing I'm not looking at him.

Except not looking at him means turning my attention to the waves lapping at the hull of the boat, rocking us back and forth gently and making me feel nauseous. Keeping the contents of my stomach in check while I spend the next hour or so squinting through my viewfinder is going to be a challenge, but there's not much I won't do for Lyric or Rob.

After I take a few test shots and adjust my settings accordingly, I give Rob a thumbs up, which lets him know we're good to start the ceremony. He really went all out for this. Apparently, he's been on the phone with the chief stewardess non-stop just to make sure everything was right, and although it's a simple set-up, it turned out beautiful. White rose petals are scattered along the teak floors of the deck, laying out the path Lyric will follow to the stern where there's a full arch with white orchids, her favorite flowers, woven through the greenery.

She has one tucked behind her ear, contrasting perfectly with her red locs that I twisted up into a semi-fancy bun before helping her into the simple, white slip dress she's wearing, and when I see her fiddling with it at the end of the aisle, I train the camera on her and snap a photo. I know they'll appreciate having candid moments like this documented just as much, if not more, as the posed photos we have planned for after the ceremony.

Rob takes his place under the arch in front of the officiant, and I turn around to focus the camera on him. He looks a little nervous, but then Jax, who's standing beside him, gives him one of those manly claps on the shoulders and says something I can't hear from where I'm standing, and he laughs. From somewhere above me, probably on the sun deck where we'll have dinner, music starts playing. Lyric lets out a soft sigh when she hears the first notes of some nineties love song, and I have to turn all the way back around just to catch her wiping the tears from her eyes as she beams at Rob.

Her fingers shake a little as she grips the bouquet, a gorgeous mix of orchids, roses, and calla lilies, and I manage to catch it on camera before she starts walking even though the image makes me think of the way my hands shook while Jax and I waited for our names to be called the day we got married at the courthouse. I push the thought away and shift my focus to Rob's face as he watches her walk towards him. From where I'm standing, I have all the integral pieces of the moment in my frame—Lyric taking steps towards her future, and Rob brushing tears away as he waits for her to make it to him—but I almost lose the shot when I see Jax in the background, looking serious, but undeniably handsome, as he stares directly at me.

Shit, not at me, *through me*. Like he knows exactly what I'm thinking and feeling in this moment. Like he saw the ghost of our wedding day flash behind my eyes even though I'm looking at him through the camera. I ignore the butterflies that take flight in my stomach and continue to click the shutter button, capturing every step Lyric takes until she's standing in front of the officiant with her eyes on Rob. They're both beaming at each other as he cups her jaw with his hand and uses one tender thumb to wipe away the tear trying to make its way down her cheek. It's such a sweet, perfect moment, and it makes my heart beat a little faster as a mix of bittersweet emotions hits me. Happiness, for these two amazing humans who somehow managed to make something beautiful out of the mess Jax and I made of our marriage. Sadness, for myself and Jax and everything we promised when we stood across from each other like our siblings are doing right now.

With love in our hearts and forever in our eyes.

The viewfinder turns blurry, and it's only then that I realize I'm crying. That despite how happy I am for my sister, this moment, *this entire week*, feels like a reminder of everything I lost. And now, with Jax within reach, asking me to take him back, and the memory of us threatening to wash away old hurt, I feel that loss more acutely than I ever have.

Focus, Amina.

Quickly, I wipe the tears in my eyes away and move closer to the arch. The officiant clears his throat and looks between Rob and Lyric, smiling at them both before he starts. His voice is deep and throaty, and even though he's speaking English, you can hear the lilt of his native tongue curling around each word. He moves through the ceremony quickly, like he's done this a million times, and before I know it, he's telling Rob he can kiss his bride. Out of the corner of my eye, I see Jax grab the officiant's elbow and pull him to the side so the moment their lips meet, in a messy kiss that's all smiles and happy sighs, there's nothing in my frame but Rob and Lyric, the setting sun and crystal blue water.

When I pull the camera away from my face and see how clean and perfect the shot is, a small spark of appreciation goes through me, and it's aimed solely at Jax and his annoyingly good memory. Because somehow, after all these years, he remembered that my biggest pet peeve as a photographer is having my shot of the kiss marred by the presence of an errant shoulder, random elbow, or in some of the most extreme cases, the entire bodies of family members who stood in front of me to capture the moment on their phone.

Most of the men I've dated since the divorce could barely remember my middle name let alone something random like that, but Jax did. And knowing that makes me feel like someone has just cracked open my chest and started the dangerous, impossible work of reshaping my heart to fit inside my ex-husband's hands.

Who am I kidding? That process started as soon as I sat down beside him on the plane. As soon as I heard him say my name for the first time in years. As soon as he told me he regretted the divorce, and the only thing that went through my mind was that I do too. Except I shouldn't regret anything because I asked for it, and I had good reasons for doing so. The best reasons, reasons no one could argue against, not even Jax.

I give myself a little shake, thankful for the internal reminder, and patch the crack in my chest back up. Reinforcing it with reminders from the night that really sealed our fate: the opening of Arcane. Because it wasn't the fight about not doing the third round of IVF that did us in, it was seeing *her* walking out of his office. Her blouse half undone, her lipstick smeared like she'd just been given the rawest, most ravenous kiss. It was the cocky arch of her brow as she walked towards me and gave me a look that said, *"Are you really surprised?"* And that wasn't even the worst thing said in that hallway.

A hand on my shoulder pulls me out of my thoughts and into the present where my sister is following her husband up the stairs to the sun deck where they'll sign their marriage certificate and sit down for their first dinner as Mr. and Mrs. Daniels.

I turn towards the person touching me, and I'm not at all surprised to see Jax at my side. His expression is soft, and his fingers are even gentler as they trail up the column of my neck and land on my cheek. Then he's rubbing his thumb over it, wiping at moisture I didn't even realize was there, and I'm leaning into his hand, for just a second before I pull back and fix my camera strap. "They need us upstairs."

I expect him to make some smart remark about me running from him again, but he doesn't say anything. He just follows me up the steps to the sundeck where Lyric and Rob are bent over the table signing the papers the officiant has put in front of them. I move around the table and take a few more pictures, and when they're done the officiant asks Jax and me, as well as two members of the crew, to sign as witnesses. Jax goes first, and when he passes the pen to me, he manages to put a world of meaning in the simple brush of our fingertips. He watches me sign my name, and it's the first time in years that I feel self-conscious about putting Amina Pierce down on paper. My cheeks are flushed as I hand the pen off and move out of the way, and Jax smiles like he knows he's affecting me.

Once all the paperwork is done, the officiant heads to the wheelhouse to chat with the captain while we eat dinner. Later, he'll leave the ship with Jax and me on a smaller boat that will take us back to the resort while Lyric and Rob stay on board. They'll be cruising around the Riviera Maya for the next three days and return to the resort just in time to greet our parents, and the rest of the guests coming in for the wedding, when they arrive on Thursday evening. I'm not loving the idea of being at the resort with no one but Jax to keep me company for the next few days, but I am eager to get off this boat and leave the newlyweds and their not-so-subtle bedroom eyes to start the first leg of their honeymoon.

We're all seated at the table, enjoying the first of several courses prepared by the yacht chef when Jax stands up and taps his wine glass with a knife. Everyone's eyes, including my reluctant ones, turn to him. He grins at each of us, but no one can miss the fact that he holds my gaze longer than anyone else's.

"I'm a little mad you guys have roped me into giving *two* speeches this week—"

Rob laughs into his wine glass. "No one asked you for this one, asshole."

"*But,*" he continues, completely undeterred by his brother's interruption. "I can't think of two people more deserving of the effort. Lyric, Rob, thank you for letting me be a part of this moment. For trusting me to bear witness to the beginning of what I know is going to be a beautiful life together. And I know you guys just got done making promises to each other, but I wanted to make some promises to you as well. As your brother and your friend, I promise to do whatever I can to protect your union. To laugh with you on the good days and cry with you on the bad. To remind you why you love each other, why you chose each other, in the moments that you want to forget. I promise not to ever let you give up on each other because this love that you've found, it's too precious to ever let go of. Trust me." He sighs, and his eyes shine with something that looks like tears as he raises his glass. "So here's to you, my brother and my sister for the second time around. We love you guys."

Lyric's eyes touch mine for just a second, and I can tell she's checking in on me to see if Jax's words affected me at all. They did, but I don't want her to know. Tonight is about her and Rob, she doesn't need to spend it worrying about me. I give her a small smile and pick up my wine glass, tilting it toward her.

"Happy wedding day, guys. We love you."

We all share a toast and spend the next hour gorging ourselves on the incredible dishes prepared by the chef. Even Jax seems impressed with the meals she's sending out, and before we board the smaller boat to leave the yacht, he heads to the kitchen with Rob to thank her for such an amazing meal. While he does that, Lyric and I stand on the deck near the boat and watch the crew prepare for our short trip back to shore.

"Are you and Jax going to be okay without us?" She asks quietly.

"I'm going to be fine, which is what your real question is."

She bumps me with her shoulder. "You didn't look all that fine when he was giving that speech. You looked like you wanted to cry."

"I did." I shrug, turning my attention back to the dark water. "But it's your wedding day, of course, I'm going to be emotional."

"Mina, it's okay if you want him back."

The words rip through me, tugging at the thoughts in my already confused mind, and I whip back around to face her so quickly it makes me feel a little queasy. "I don't—"

Lyric grips my hand, earnest eyes on mine. "I know you're scared. That's why I didn't want to say anything, but I see the way you look at him. I see the way he looks at you, and I just think maybe it's worth it to try."

"Do you really want to spend your wedding night playing marriage counselor?"

"No. I want to spend my wedding night making sure my baby sister is just as happy as I am. You love him, Mina, and I know he still loves you. The way things ended with you guys never made any sense…"

"It didn't have to make sense to you, Lyric." My voice is cold, stiff, and I can feel a flare of annoyance my sister doesn't deserve to have pointed her way building in my chest. It's not her fault I never told anyone about how I had my heart ripped out of my chest and stomped on that night. I mean I could have. I could have *destroyed* him, laid all the blame for our shattered marriage at his feet, but that wasn't exactly the case. I was responsible too, and maybe I didn't cheat, but I did neglect him. I did push him away. I did put all of my energy and hope into getting pregnant, into the next round of IVF, into the next blood test. And when it really came down to it, to looking at Cassidy and her stupid eyebrow and its unspoken question, the only word echoing in my mind was no.

No, I wasn't surprised, but I was ashamed, and that shame was private. Something raw and ugly and not fit to be shared with anyone, not even Jax. I blow out a steadying breath and squeeze her fingers, which are still wrapped tightly around mine, before releasing her. "Let's not get into this tonight. I'm sure Rob is somewhere around here waiting to drag you into bed."

As if on cue, I hear Rob and Jax's voices filtering through the air, sounding clipped and tense. It's clear they're moving towards us and it's not long before they're joining us on the deck, their body language reflecting the tension I heard a second ago. The engine for the smaller boat is running, all of the navigational lights are on and one of the two crew members tasked with taking us back is helping the officiant onboard.

Rob grabs Lyric up by her waist and drops a kiss on her shoulder. "Say goodnight, wife, it's time for us to go to bed."

I fake gag, and Jax frowns at his brother. "Ugh. Could you at least wait until we're gone?"

"I would," Rob says, already dragging a giggling Lyric away from us. "But you're not leaving fast enough."

I shake my head at my playful brother-in-law and his blushing bride and start towards the boat. "Good night, guys."

Jax scoffs and climbs on the boat after me, settling himself in the seat across from me with a small bag in his left hand. I watch his fingers curl around the brown paper, studying each one and lingering, stupidly, on his ring finger. Where he used to wear the symbol of our love. Where a thin silver band used to tell everyone that looked at him he belonged to me.

It didn't stop him from betraying you, though.

My heart clenches, and fresh tears spring, blurring my vision. I cross my arms over my chest and shift in my seat until I'm facing the side of the boat. The wind whips around my face, scooping up my tears and carrying them away.

6

Jax

The ride back to the resort is a quick one, and I'm thankful it is because I know how much Amina hates boats. I'm honestly impressed she got through the ride to the anchorage spot earlier today, the ceremony, and dinner without barfing on someone or something. I thought the ride back might be a little precarious, so I got some motion sickness pills, crackers, and ginger ale from the chief stewardess while she and Lyric were talking, but we make it all the way to shore without her turning green.

When we get to the dock, Amina is the first one off, and I leave the bag with all the things I got for her—things she doesn't need—on my seat, so I can run to catch up with her. She didn't say anything to me the entire way back, and it's not lost on me that she's running from me again. It's not exactly surprising that she is. This is our first time being truly alone since what happened in the cabana earlier, and I know she's probably still reeling from the wedding and shocked she let me so close, so quickly. All of her instincts must be screaming at her to get as far away from me, as fast as she can, so she can have some time to shore up her resolve, but I have no intentions of letting that happen. I wait until we've made it back to the villas before I speak.

"Let's get a drink."

I say it casually, like it doesn't matter to me one way or another if she agrees, but we both know it does. She turns to look at me, brow furrowed in confusion, but she doesn't stop walking towards her door. I follow behind her just like I did last night and just being in the same space where she first let me touch her, sends a thrum of awareness through me.

"We've just spent the last few hours drinking. Why would I want to do that?"

"So I can have a little more time to convince you to spend the night in my bed."

Her steps grind to a halt, and suddenly she's turning around and slapping me in my chest. It's supposed to hurt, but all my body registers is that she's touching me.

"I'm not in the mood for your jokes, Jax."

The wobble in her voice wipes the cocky smile I'm sporting right off my face, and before I know it I'm reaching for her. Pulling her into my arms and remembering the single tear slipping down her cheek as she watched Lyric and Rob finish their first kiss as husband and wife. I knew today would be hard for her because it was hard for me too. Like waking up on Christmas day and having to watch someone open the present you spent all year begging for. But that's all the more reason for us to be together right now. I'm the only one who understands what she's feeling. That bittersweet mix of happiness for the people you love and unyielding sadness for yourself.

We've navigated this space too many times to count. Every time one of our friends announced that they were expecting while we prayed for double lines that never came. Every time we shopped for a present for a baby shower and swallowed the disappointment that we weren't in those aisles searching for the perfect outfit to bring our baby home in.

In all of those times, we had each other. Amina would bury her face in my neck and let it all just wash over her, the good, the bad, the bitter, all of it rushing like rivers of pain over my skin. That river is flowing now, a quiet current of unexpected grief soaking into my shirt as she sniffles against my skin. And I don't even need to ask because I know that these tears are for us.

"It's okay, baby." My words threaten to shatter the moment, to remind her that leaning on me goes directly against her plan to put some distance between us, but I can't help it. I want her to know that I've got her, that I understand. "I'm right here. Tell me what you need."

She pulls back to look at me and panic grips me as I silently pray I haven't fucked this up already. Her bottom lip trembles, and she sinks her teeth into it to stop the motion. And I must be feeling rather brave because as soon as she does, I reach up and use my thumb to free the flesh from its cage.

"These aren't some sad 'no one is ever going to love me' maid of honor tears."

"I know that." *Because I love you. Because I've always loved you.*

The words don't make it out of my mouth, but I let them show on my face, and I know she sees them when those flashes of copper in her eyes burn brighter, blinding me with their disagreement. My lips part, ready to put words to our silent argument, but I snap them closed. If I start an argument with her, then I won't find out where this little speech is going.

"And this isn't some cliche night of the wedding hook up between the maid of honor and the best man."

Oh. All of the blood in my body rushes straight to my groin in response to the phrase 'hook up' coming out of her mouth. And all at once, I'm hit with a thousand images of us together. Of those same lips wrapped around my dick. Of those same eyes rolling into the back of her head as I move inside her, hitting all of her spots. The ones I know so well. The ones I didn't think I'd get to feel again in this lifetime.

I nod, trying, and probably failing, not to look like a teenage boy being told he can put his dick somewhere other than the palm of his hand. "Got it."

Amina steps back, looking certain of herself, of what we're about to do. "I'm not going to be waking up in your bed, Jax. This is a one-time thing. You'll help me forget that I'm a terrible person for being jealous of my sister's happiness, and I'll give you the gift of my body and enough memories to get you through the rest of your life, so you can let go of this ridiculous notion that we should get back together. No spending the night. And as soon as you leave my bed we'll go back to being a normal divorced couple."

"With married siblings?" It's the only question I can ask because it's the only part of what she just said that makes sense. Everything else, but especially the part about me wanting us to get back together being ridiculous, gets pushed down into a box and shoved into the furthest part of my brain.

She nods. "Yes. A normal divorced couple with married siblings."

I bite my lip to stifle the laugh trying to break free from my chest because laughing right now, when Amina looks so beautifully serious, would just be rude. Still, it's cute that she thinks we will be able to walk away from each other if we do this tonight. It doesn't matter how many safeguards or parameters we put on this thing, if we start this, there will be no ending it.

"Amina." My hands go to her waist, pulling her hips forward so she's pressed into my erection. Her pupils dilate, copper and brown giving way to endless pools of black. "I'm happy to help you forget everything but the way my dick feels when I'm moving inside of you, but I just want to be clear on something." I lean down and let my lips brush the lobe of her ear. She shivers against me. "When we do this, it changes *everything*. There's no going back to normal or pretending that this never happened."

Her brows dip inward as she considers my words. "So you're saying you don't want to have sex with me tonight? Because if you can't agree to my terms then it's not happening."

"Oh, no. I'm going to fuck you tonight, baby. And I'm going to do it so thoroughly you're going to wonder why you spent so much time fighting with me about something that's an inevitability."

"Because it's not an inevitability. It's *you* assuming that I'll want more than one night in bed with you, and *me* disabusing you of the notion."

I study her face, noting her resolute expression and the stubborn tilt of her chin. Every second I spend arguing with her takes me further away from the reality of her in my arms, and that's the last thing I want. I sigh. "How do I change your mind?"

"You don't."

"Can I at least suggest an amendment?"

She shrugs. "Sure."

"Give me more than tonight. We'll be alone here for the next three days. Spend them with me. Let me show you how serious I am about you, about *us*."

Amina looks panicked and uncertain, but she hasn't pushed me away yet, so I guess that must mean she's considering my proposal. "Jax, I don't know..."

"If you're not convinced by the time everyone gets here for the wedding, then I'll leave it alone. But you have to give me a chance, Mina. I need some time, where I'm not chasing you around this damn resort, to prove myself to you. When you walked away all those years ago, I let you go way too easily. And now I have to work my ass off to make it right, but that's okay because I'm not afraid of hard work. Not if it gets me you."

7

Amina

I'm not afraid of hard work. Not if it gets me you.

God damn Jaxon Daniels and his perfect mouth that says perfect things. Things I feel like I've waited a lifetime to hear. Things that threaten to wipe away every trace of pain caused by his betrayal. Things that make me want to tear every shred of clothing off of him with my bare hands and fuck him on the threshold of my villa without a care in the world about who might see.

Breathe, Amina. Breathe and tell him this was a mistake. That you didn't mean to open this door because you're not sure if you're strong enough to walk through it.

My lips part, and I lick them because suddenly they feel dry. Jax tracks the movement with his eyes. There's a desperate hunger there, one that reminds me of what it's like to be devoured by him, loved by him, worshiped by him. And God help me, but I want to experience that feeling again. Even if it's just for three days.

"Okay."

His brows shoot up, nearly reaching his hairline and drawing my attention to the curls I've been dying to sink my fingers into since I spotted him at the airport yesterday. Have we really only been here a day? Shock courses through me, some of it due to the realization that it took Jax no time at all to suck me back into the madness that is us, but the rest of it is due to the word that just left my mouth.

I've just agreed to sleep with him. To have a three-day fling with my ex-husband who has made it clear he wants it to be more. My pulse pounds at the thought. *More.* The offer is tempting, especially when I thought the only thing there would ever be between us was history—regret, heartbreak, and maybe some nieces and nephews if Lyric ever decides to have kids—I never thought we'd have a future.

"Open the door, Mina."

Jax's face is mere inches from mine, and whatever shock he felt at hearing my agreement is gone. Dissolved by the heat in his eyes. Demolished by the sparks of electricity pinging between us, filling up the tiny walkway. I can almost taste his desire. It's there, in the air between us, thicker than the humid breeze trying to move between our fused bodies.

I have the fleeting thought to reach out and touch it, to try and capture it in my hands and remind myself that it's real, but Jax shatters it when he clears his throat and gives me an expectant look. Momentary disappointment slips down my spine at his calm and patient demeanor. I had expected the seconds before we dived into this madness to be a blur, a flurry of movement and thoughtless action, but this is different.

This is slow and intentional, but no less passionate. This is intense and purposeful and everything I do, including surrendering to the calm order he's just given me by digging my key card out of my purse, is fraught with meaning. Laced with reminders that I'm choosing this, choosing him.

My fingers wrap around the key card, and I watch Jax, watch me pull it out. He's so calm, so completely in control of himself and this moment, almost like he planned for us to end up here, just like this. *Maybe he did.* And maybe I always knew it would happen too. Maybe I hoped for it in the deepest, darkest part of me. In that far chamber of my heart that's gone unused since my last name became Pierce again, but seems to be brimming with forgiveness and hope right now.

I spin around in Jax's loose hold on my waist and press the key card to the electronic pad. The light goes from red to green just like it did last night, and before I can overthink it, I push the door open and walk into the cool, quiet of the villa with Jax behind me. As soon as we're inside, he releases me, and I move deeper into the room. I can feel his eyes on me as I set my camera bag and purse down in a chair at the small dining table by the window. I allow myself one steadying breath before I turn back around to face him. He's still standing by the door, his hands in his pockets and his eyes still on me, watching me quietly as I kick off my heels and prepare to release my hair from the bun I've had it in all day. I've just put my fingers on the first bobby pin when Jax finally finds his words.

"Wait." He pushes off of the door, crossing the room with a few strides of his long, powerful legs, and stopping in front of me. "Let me."

My arms drop to my sides as an echo of our past ripples through me. Nights of sitting between his legs while he released my hair from the fancy, twisted buns I'd do for whatever wedding I shot that day. "Okay."

His hands go to my shoulders, and I let him turn me around. My pelvis bumps the table as he moves in close to me, pressing his hips to my ass so I can feel that he's even harder now than he was a few minutes ago. A small moan leaves my lips, and I'm not sure if it's because of the feel of his erection against me or because of his fingers making short work of removing the bobby pins digging into my scalp.

Messy tendrils of curls fall down, grazing my shoulders as Jax releases them one by one. I don't know where the pins disappear to, and I don't have time to worry too much about it because once they're gone Jax is unraveling the loose twists that made up the bun, and the feel of his fingers sliding through the dense strands of my hair has my scalp prickling with anticipation. The memory of the way his fingers felt sinking into it, rubbing and soothing the skin, unearths itself and is given new life when it happens in the present.

I moan again, and this time I know exactly what the cause is. It's the reverent, yet almost painful, glide of his rough fingertips through my hair. It's the gentle kneading of flesh over bone. It's the sharp and sudden sensation of rightness as he touches me like I belong to him, like I've always belonged to him, and the surge of agreement that floods my body. That tells him 'yes, I do belong to you' with every moan he draws from my lips and the subtle rolling of my hips, dragging my ass across an erection that I know is just for me. That, even now with my doubts about his intentions and the rising panic flaring in the back of my mind, I crave to take into my body and never let go.

Jax withdraws his fingers from my hair, and I would be sad about the loss if I wasn't so distracted by the way they're brushing wild curls off of my shoulder to make space for his lips on my neck. I arch against him, craning my neck to one side to offer him more, and crying out when he goes from gentle kisses to a hot, open mouth suckling that makes me feel like I'm being swallowed whole.

My eyes fall shut as his hands move up my arms, trailing up my shoulders until his fingers find the straps of my dress. I'm not wearing a bra, so when he slides the straps down, sending the flimsy fabric into a free fall down my body, the cool air hits my bare skin, and my nipples tighten instantly. Jax lets out a sound that's somewhere between a growl and a moan as he palms my breasts, pinching the pebbled skin as he lifts his mouth from my neck.

"I want to bend you over this table and fuck you until you can't see straight. Can I?"

I don't even have to think twice about my answer. After all, this is why we're here. This is why I'm undoing two years worth of learning to live without his touch. "*Yes.*"

The question might as well have been rhetorical because his hands are leaving my breasts, skating over my belly and around my waist to grip the band of my thong well before the answer passes my lips. Then he's pushing it down and dropping to his knees to follow its descent with his mouth, raining kisses over the dimples in my back, pausing to take a firm bite out of one of my ass cheeks and finally stopping around my ankles.

He taps my leg, and I step out, simultaneously hating myself for heedlessly following his silent order and loving how it feels like nothing has changed between us. I mean I know time has passed, that I've been with other people and he has too, but right now it feels like he's always been mine, and I know I've always been his. Right now, it feels easy to believe him when he says he shouldn't have let me go, when he says he'll fight to get me back, when he says he loves me.

He hasn't said that yet.

Not with his mouth, no. But with his eyes. With his hands. With his lips on my skin...

"Bend over, baby," Jax says. He's still kneeling on the ground behind me, but he's up right now, with his face inches from the swollen lips of my sex. He doesn't wait for me to comply, even though I have every intention of doing so. That's how it is with me and him, how it's always been, he gives an order and I submit. I give him my trust, and he shows me why he's the only man who's ever been able to give me *this*. Complete and utter freedom. From making decisions and taking care of responsibilities. From thinking of anything besides the way my body feels under his expert touch. No one I've been with since the divorce has been able to make me feel like this. All those men have been too busy battling insecurities created by my professional success and smart mouth to do what Jax has managed to do in just a few minutes.

His hand lands on the small of my back, guiding me down to the table until my cheek hits the cool wood. Against my heated skin, it almost feels like too much, but I can't move now. He won't let me, and, more importantly, I don't want to.

"Spread your legs for me. I want to see all of you." A shiver wracks me as moisture pools between my legs. Moisture I'm putting on display for him when I widen my stance. Jax sucks in a sharp breath, and I smile to myself because that sound belongs to me. "Is it possible that you've gotten even more beautiful?"

"I—"

Lose every thought in my head and every word I've ever known as he uses his hands to spread me open and buries his face in my pussy, breathing deeply before treating me to a decadent swipe of his tongue. It's a long, torturous glide of his flesh over mine, and I rise up on my tip-toes and scream because it feels so fucking good—better than the cabana, better than anything has felt in years—and I know I'm going to come apart for him in seconds. Fresh tears blur my vision, but I don't care. I don't need to see, all I need to do is feel him. The fingers of one of his hands hold me open for him while the others move down to play the in the moisture slipping out of me.

Jax pulls back, trading his mouth for his busy hand and letting his thumb sink into me while his middle finger reaches forward and lands on my clit. His technique would strike me as odd if I didn't know him so well, but I do know him, and I know exactly what he's going to do next. The thought alone has my walls rippling, the beginning of what's sure to be an intense orgasm building in my core.

Sharp teeth sink into the back of my thigh. "Don't come."

I whimper, irritation sparks in my chest at the order, but I can feel the orgasm fading as my body responds to him without my permission. "You said you were going to bend me over and fuck me until I can't see straight. Not tease me and deny me an orgasm."

"Are you that desperate to have my dick inside you again?"

"Your dick. Your fingers. It doesn't really matter as long as I get to *come*."

A dark chuckle fills the air. "You're such a desperate little liar."

His thumb presses down, massaging my g-spot. My thighs tense, and my eyes roll into the back of my head. Jax keeps the pressure steady and perfect, so I'm climbing and climbing, my blood pounding in my veins and my walls clutching at him until I'm sure I'm going to go over with no regard for his order not to.

"Jax!" It's a warning and a plea and a sob all wrapped up in one. A broken and thready sound that makes him growl against my skin as he removes his thumb from my soaked channel and replaces it with his middle and index finger. I don't have time to process the invasion because then he's dragging that thumb up the seam of my ass, using the juices of my arousal to circle my other entrance. And although I knew it was coming, I still feel my mouth go slack when he presses down, inching his way inside of me slowly. "*Oh...*"

"That's right." Jax whispers, pumping in and out of my ass with slow, shallow thrusts that I can't even move to meet. It just feels too good. Too perfect. Too right. "Lie and say you don't miss me now, Mina. Tell me you haven't dreamed about spreading your legs for me, taking everything I have to give you."

His words skate across my skin, sending goosebumps up my spine, and I'm moaning so loudly now I'm sure anyone walking by can hear me screaming for him. "I'm going to come, Jax." My walls clench again, punctuating my words.

"Not until you have my dick buried deep inside you."

Rising to his feet, he takes the hand he was using to hold me open and uses it to pull his dick out of his pants. God, I wish I could see him right now. I wish I could turn around and drop to my knees, pull him into my mouth, and suck him dry. *Later.* I promise myself. *Later I'll drive him just as crazy as he's driving me.* He pulls his fingers out of my sex, but his thumb is still in my ass as he drags his dick through my slick folds. I rock my hips back, trying to capture even an inch of his rock-hard length.

"Hurry."

He slaps my ass with his free hand, punishing me for being impatient even though he likes me this way. Desperate and begging for him, wanting nothing more than to give myself over to the wave of madness cresting inside of me. And it *is* madness. Everything about this moment is. From the heavy, full feeling in my ass where Jax's thumb is still working at me, to the shock waves of anticipation in my core that make me feel like my entire body is a building ready for demolition, and Jax is the wrecking ball.

"*Please.*"

He's notched at my entrance now, rocking back and forth on his heels to tease me with the possibility of our joining, and I bite my lip to stop myself from doing something stupid like begging. But my hips don't stop moving, my body doesn't stop seeking his out, and he doesn't stop teasing me. Doesn't stop driving me crazy with the one digit working deep inside of me and the maddening pressure of the others digging into my skin wherever they can.

Jax makes another pass through my folds and groans. "I don't have a condom, Amina." I freeze, wondering why on Earth he would say something like that right now. Especially when it's the farthest thing from my mind because I can't remember the last time we used one. *That was years ago though, and we've both been with other people.*

"I don't—" I swallow against the painful knot that's suddenly taken up residence in my throat. "I'm clean, Jax. I haven't been with anyone in months."

My cheeks burn. I never thought I would have to say those words to him. Never thought the list of people I've slept with would comprise of anyone but him. Never thought I would have to think too hard about how he added a name to his list while he still belonged to me. I feel him lean forward, covering my back with his body, pressing a kiss to my shoulder, and sending the painful thought back where it came from.

"It's been over a year for me, and I've always..."

I close my eyes. I don't want to hear him finish that sentence. "I trust you."

Do I trust him though? Or do I just want him to make this empty feeling in my chest go away? Does it even matter?

Jax stands back up, and the head of his dick is back at my entrance. "Hold on to the table, baby."

No, it doesn't matter if I trust him. The only thing that matters is this.

My heart lurches as I scramble to reach the edges of the table. As soon as my fingers find purchase on the smooth wood, I feel Jax rear back and slam forward, nearly upending the table with the force of his thrust. My feet leave the ground, and if I wasn't already halfway laying on the table, *that* would have put me flat on my face.

"God!" I scream, holding tighter to the wood while Jax bruises me with his grip. His thumb has gone still, no longer working at me but still providing the exquisite sensation of fullness, and honestly, that's fine because adding anything else to the feeling of his dick stretching me out might be too much right now.

Especially now that he's moving. Slow, deep strokes that are supposed to feel lazy, almost thoughtless, but I know are meant to drive me insane. This is how I like it. How he taught me to like it. With every inch of him dragging over the most sensitive parts of me, tossing gasoline on the fire burning inside my core. Pulling pleasure from every nerve ending, setting off an avalanche that won't be stopped, won't be deterred.

"You're still mine." He says, sounding awestruck. Like he can't believe that the time we've spent apart hasn't erased his claim on my body. I open my mouth, but no words come out, which is just as well because there's nothing I can say in response. I mean, I guess I could try to disagree, but it would be pretty hard to argue with my ass in the air and his various appendages invading my body. "You'll always be mine, Mina."

The emotion curling around his words makes my fucking chest hurt. I don't want it. I don't want him to say these things, not now when I'm too lost in the feel of him moving inside of me to fight against the feelings it stirs up. When I left him, I was numb, but now I feel everything. I've *been* feeling everything. The ever-present heartbreak. The old hurt and new anger. Especially anger. Because I don't understand how his words can match my heart. *My heart*—stupid, treacherous organ that it is—that has longed for this very moment since I knew this week was happening. That is now wondering why we couldn't be this in sync when it really mattered. When it could have saved us.

"Just shut up and fuck me."

The words leave my mouth in an angry, tangled ball of syllables, but once Jax unravels them he growls and pulls his finger out of my ass. I yelp, surprised at the sudden loss of fullness there, but he doesn't acknowledge the sound. He's too focused on using both of his hands to grip my waist and yank me down the table until nothing but my elbows are resting on the wooden surface. His fingertips dig into my skin, and I moan my approval. I need him rough because any more of his tenderness might destroy me. The change in position allows me to place more of my weight on my feet, and I use the leverage to rock against him. Bouncing my ass and teasing both of us while he pushes out a frustrated breath through his nose.

I expect him to take over, to give me some of those angry, feral strokes that will send us both hurtling towards the finish line, but he doesn't. He just lets me keep going, impaling myself on his length while giving me nothing but the pleasure of using him. I work myself into a frenzy, moaning and cursing as I fuck myself with his dick and too lost to the pleasure rolling through me to notice that after my little outburst, he's stopped fucking me altogether. He's still holding my waist but letting me control the rhythm, and it's not long before my orgasm descends. It's everything I knew it would be. Heated sparks slipping down my spine, electric pulses in my core, all the makings of a groundbreaking release that's so close I can almost taste it. My eyes fall shut and my movements lose any semblance of a rhythm as my thighs tense, and my walls clench around him.

"Oh, God." My back arches and every muscle in my body tightens as the sensation intensifies. "I'm com—"

Suddenly, my core is empty, clenching around nothing as the building pressure low in my belly dissipates. It feels like it slips away slowly, but in the second it takes me to turn around and figure out what the hell has happened, it's gone. What's back is my anger, only it's turned into a dangerous kind of rage, and it's aimed squarely at the man standing in front of me like he didn't just ruin the best part of my day.

He grins at me, and it's an evil, impish grin, that somehow reminds me he's done everything today but kiss me. I push the thought away, honing in on the frustration mixing with the desire still burning through me.

"What the fuck?!" I march towards him, and he doesn't move. Doesn't even flinch as I approach him in all my naked glory. My body's changed since we were last together. I'm a little thicker around the waist and thighs, my stomach has a few new stretch marks, and my breasts are fuller than they've ever been, but I don't feel the least bit shy in front of him. Probably because I know my body is fabulous and he still looks at me like I'm the only meal he ever wants to eat. That's exactly how he's looking at me right now, with that stupid grin on his face and all of his clothes in place save for the part of his waistband that's dipping under the weight of his balls. The sight of which almost makes me lose track of my anger because my mouth starts watering with the need to taste myself on him. "Why would you do that?"

"Because you needed to be reminded of the way things are between us."

I roll my eyes. "Up until a few minutes ago, there wasn't even an us."

His eyes flash, sparkling with possession and humor. "There's never been a world where there wasn't an us."

My chest splits open again. A well of emotion leaking out and swallowing everything it touches. "Can you at least make good on your promise before you start saying shit like that again?"

"No." He laughs as he starts to get undressed. Toeing off his shoes, yanking his shirt over his head to expose the slabs of hard muscle making up his torso and chest, and finally pushing his pants down his legs and stepping out of them. I swallow, *hard*, completely in awe of the sight of him fully naked. "You need to accept that me saying 'shit like that' is a part of this. Once you do, I'll make good on my promise. Get on your knees."

I blink, stunned at the sudden change of direction. "What?"

He sits down on the edge of my bed, legs spread wide. His dick—long and thick with beautifully brutal veins along the shaft and a wide, flared tip—curves proudly towards his rigid abs with the smallest bit of precum glistening on the head. Again, my mouth waters at the thought of tasting him, of tasting us. "On your knees, baby. You want my dick in your mouth."

On its own volition, my tongue makes a quick pass over my lips, and Jax lifts his brows in triumph. I hate that he can still read me so easily. "And you want a way to stop me from telling you to shut up while you're pouring your heart out like a love-sick teenager."

He laughs, and it's the most perfect sound. Rich and deep and gravelly. Warm like the sun was today when it was at its highest point in the sky. "That's an added bonus. Truthfully though, I've wanted your lips wrapped around my dick since you called me Jaxon on the plane."

"That was just yesterday." I remind him, lips quirking at the happy little coincidence that no doubt played a role in landing us here. I'm moving towards him now, taking small steps towards the edge of the bed, my knees already begging to bend for him.

Jax tracks my steps without his eyes ever leaving my face. "I know, and a day was still too long to wait for you."

"I wasn't even supposed to be in first class," I admit, standing in front of him now. His hands go to my waist, managing to give me the barest hint of a squeeze before I sink to the ground. I have to tilt my chin up to look at him, to see the hunger and pride and possession in the rings of smoke and quartz that are his eyes. "I guess it's a good thing Lyric upgraded my ticket."

"She didn't."

Surprise sends my brows towards my hairline. "What? Then how?"

"I had your ticket changed." He brushes some of my curls over my shoulder and away from my face. "My goal for this trip was to come back with your

63

heart, Mina. You've always had mine, but I knew I was going to have to put everything I had into reclaiming yours. I knew you weren't going to make it easy on me, and I was prepared to use everything to my advantage. The romantic atmosphere, the emotions from the wedding, the proximity of our villas. Everything. And then I saw you at the airport, and I knew I couldn't wait to start the process of winning you back. So I called my assistant, gave her all of your info, and got you the last seat in first class. The one by me."

It's unnerving. The sincerity in his tone. The determined glint in his eyes. The solemn truth playing across his features. I came to Tulum thinking of all the ways I could avoid this man, all the ways I could protect myself from the hurt I've been living with for years, and Jax was wracking his brain to figure out how to get us here.

"You're crazy."

"For you." And I must be crazy too because I believe him. Even with the pain of our past lingering between us, I believe that he wants this. That he wants me. I just wish I believed it was enough to save us from repeating our past mistakes. Jax slips a finger under my chin, lifting it so that my bewildered gaze meets his serious one. "You're thinking too much, baby. All I need you to do is feel."

One of his hands snakes around to the back of my head and sinks into my curls. Gathering them in a tight ponytail that's as restrictive as it is satisfying. Every follicle on my scalp tingles, and it's only slightly painful, just enough to push all the anxiety out of my body and invite desire back in. I pull in a clarifying breath and lick my lips.

Jax smiles, and it's a dark, perfect thing that makes my blood sing. "*Open.*"

My lips part and then separate completely as he uses his hold on my hair to guide my head towards his waiting erection. The sharp and tangy mixture of us explodes on my tongue as I pull him into my mouth, and I moan at the taste. With his assistance, I've managed to capture most of his length on the first try, but I want more.

"That's it, baby," Jax mutters, pulling me back up. He does a quick scan of my face, making sure I'm okay before pushing me back down. I sheath my teeth with my lips and relax my throat, intent on taking every inch of him

64

this time. He hisses when I'm successful. "You look so good with your lips wrapped around my dick."

His praise, combined with the depravity of him holding my head down while he fucks into the heated suction of my mouth, has the pressure building in my womb again. I reach down between my legs and find my clit swollen and sensitive; it would take less than one flick of my finger over the bud to set me off, but I don't want to come like that. I want what Jax promised me earlier, his dick buried deep inside of me while my walls milk him for every drop of cum.

I let out a desperate moan as I remove my hand from my cleft and place it on Jax's thigh. Nails scoring into his skin as I flutter my tongue over his crown and swallow a pearl of precum. It's the first in a semi-steady stream that tells me Jax is close, close enough to be slowing the once frenzied movements of his hips and dragging my lips up his shaft by the grip he has on my hair. We're both panting when our eyes meet. Both on the edge of madness because of stalled orgasms and the burning need to not only come but reclaim each other.

"Come here."

He releases my hair and offers me his hand, the same one that was just tangled in my curls, and pulls me up onto the bed with him. Somehow I bypass his lap and end up on my back with him on top of me. Both of his arms are planted on either side of my head, and my legs are spread wide to accommodate the width of his hips. It's the same position we were in on the sofa in the cabana. Jax leans in close, brushing his lips over mine, and reminding me once again that we haven't kissed yet. The thought makes me laugh.

"We're doing everything backward."

"What do you mean?" His dick is back, nudging against my entrance and meeting no resistance because I'm so fucking wet it's probably soaking through the bedding underneath us.

I rock into him. He sucks in a sharp breath, pupils dilating further even though they're already blown. "You're about to have your dick in me for the second time tonight, but you haven't even kissed me yet."

"I was waiting on *you* to kiss *me*."

I gasp, and it has less to do with his words and more to do with the feel of him sliding inside of me. Inch by breathtaking inch until he's buried deep. "*Ohhhh.*"

"So do it." He's moving now, in a powerful but even rhythm that's going to undo me in no time, and the words are lost beneath the waves of pleasure washing over me. He brings his lips to my ear and sinks his teeth into the lobe. "Amina. Did you hear what I said?"

"No." My voice is barely a whisper. My arms are wrapped around him, fingertips digging into his skin in a manner that can only be described as desperate. I clear my throat, trying to speak clearly, to not sound so damn wrecked by the weight of his body pressing me into the mattress. "No."

"I want you to kiss me. I *need* you to kiss me, baby."

I'm nodding even though at the moment I don't know why it matters who kisses who first. All I know is that Jax needs something from me, and he's asking me for it. Something precious, something important that I can give him. That I can't fail at or mess up.

"Okay." I bring my hands to his face, both of them cradling his strong jaw and guiding him back to my mouth. He comes willingly, still pumping into me at that steady tempo that has my legs quivering, and his eyes burn into me as his lips hover just over mine. Every muscle in his face is still—quiet, expectant—waiting for me to move, reminding me of the fourteen-year-old boy whose face morphed into a mask of shock and horror when I grabbed it with both hands and subjected us both to the most embarrassing first kiss Skateland, the local skating rink, had ever seen. That was our first kiss, and he didn't speak to me for a week afterward because he was under the impression that guys should always make the first move and was mad that I beat him to the punch.

Now, he's asking me to initiate this first, *again.* And there's something beautifully poetic about him giving me the honor. He watches me closely, and I see the moment he realizes that I get what he's doing. A sneaky little smile tugs on the corners of his lips, and I can't hold out any longer. I lift up and crush my lips to his, sighing because he tastes like me, and I taste like us. Moaning because the second our lips touch he takes over the kiss, plundering my mouth with his tongue and somehow making the strokes match the tempo

66

he's set with his hips.

Screaming because when those tell-tale ripples of pleasure start to roll through me, he doesn't stop kissing me or fucking me, he keeps going. Sliding his lips over mine, swallowing my relieved cries brimming with pleasure, and slamming into me over and over again until he collapses with his own guttural groans that reverberate through me.

8

Jax

My wife's lips are pillow-soft. Plump little cushions made for kissing and licking and capturing between my teeth while I have one hand wrapped around her throat, fingers digging into the sides of her neck, and my hips cradled between her thighs with my dick nestled as far inside of her as it can go. I wish I could go deeper.

I wish I could climb underneath her skin. Burrow into her heart, make her soul my home.

Amina wraps her legs around my waist, pulling me closer like she can hear my thoughts. A throaty moan vibrates against my palm, and even though I spent all of last night hearing them, it still makes my dick twitch inside of her. I growl and release her bottom lip.

"Keep making sounds like that, and I'm going to have to keep you in bed all day."

"Wasn't that the plan?" She gasps, biting her own lip now.

"No, I was going to be a gentleman and let you recover from last night."

But then I woke up and saw her. Her hair wild and tussled, spread out over the white pillowcases and tickling my arm. Her cheek pressed to my chest, one arm thrown over my stomach and a leg tangled between mine. She was glorious. Beautiful. And all mine.

I woke her up with her legs on my shoulders and my tongue in her pussy. She still tasted like us, that perfect mixture of her juices and my cum dripping out of her, reminding me of the countless times she let me finish inside her. It didn't take long for her to wake up, fire in her sleepy eyes, my name on her lips, and early morning sunlight caressing her skin. The moment I heard it, I climbed up her body and kissed her while my dick took advantage of the moisture we created together to slip inside, savoring every inch she surrendered to me. I don't know how much time has passed since then—minutes, hours, days—or how many orgasms we've had between us, but we're going to have to get some new sheets or move to my villa once this is done.

"You've never been a gentleman." Her brows fall together as I pull back as far as her locked ankles will let me and drive back into her again. *"Deeper, Jax."*

Reaching around me with my free hand, I force her legs from around my hips and rear back, nearly leaving her softness before slamming forward. Amina's eyes go wide, and her lips part but no words come out. Just a gentle woosh of breath that tells me everything and nothing. I want to ask her a million questions and tell her a thousand truths. I want to kiss her lips and know every thought in her mind.

"Is that deep enough, baby?" I drop a kiss to her lips, and when I pull away to gaze into her eyes, she tries to follow me up like she doesn't want the kiss to end. "Can you feel me everywhere yet?" I loosen my grip on her neck, letting my hand trail down her smooth skin until it's right over her pounding heart. "Can you feel me here?"

She doesn't answer. I don't expect her to; she can't admit it yet, and that's okay. I move my hands further down her body, grab one of her legs under her knee and push it up until her foot is perched on my shoulder. Then I twist my hips, angling my strokes to give her the full sensation of me hitting the deepest part of her. She must be sore, or at least a little tender because I feel her stiffen momentarily. I start to slow my strokes, but she shakes her head.

"No, don't you dare stop. It's so fucking good."

The last thing I want to do is disappoint her, I'll die before I do that again, so I push her leg back further and give her everything. Sweat drips down my back as I drive into her with force and strength I shouldn't have after last night and this morning. With anyone else, I would be done after the first few rounds, but with Amina, *for Amina*, I'm tireless. Her breasts bounce with every thrust, and I make a note to pay special attention to them at some point.

"I'm going to fuck those." My gaze flits to her chest, and her eyes dance with amusement and mischief when she sees what has my attention.

"These?" She runs her hands up her torso, palming the supple flesh that has me mesmerized and kneading them with a smile teasing the corner of her lips.

"Yes." I'm trying to keep my voice even but watching her give her breasts the same rough squeezes I would give them has my throat tightening and my strokes growing jerky. "And you're going to hold them together for me. I'll let you play with your nipples while I fuck them just like I'm fucking your pussy right now."

"Mhmm." She purses her lips, a faux considerate expression taking over her face as she rolls her nipples between her fingers. "And what if I say they're off-limits?"

The idea of any part of her being off-limits to me is laughable, yet infuriating. A wave of possessiveness rolls down my spine. I drop her leg and swipe her fingers away. Her eyes widen as I come down on her, covering her luscious breasts with my sweaty chest.

"I've had my dick, my fingers, and tongue in every single part of you but that's where you draw the line?" I press down harder, rubbing my sweat into her skin and increasing the tempo of my thrusts, turning it into a grinding, pistoning of my hips that has her walls clamping down on me. She's close. "*Is that where you draw the line, baby?*"

"No...it's not."

"Damn right, it's not." I nuzzle into the open space in her neck and lap up the sweat dotting her skin. Her thighs quiver. "You're going to let me have you wherever I want, however I want."

"*Yes.*"

I'm slamming into her now with strokes that can't be called smooth by any stretch of the imagination, and we're both standing on the edge of a cliff. Glancing over the edge and looking forward to the fall. Amina turns her head into my arm, mouth opening on a moan while her chest heaves and her body clutches at me, causing my balls to tighten fiercely. I lift up a little, giving myself just enough space to reach between us and stroke her clit, pushing her to her release, so I can finally give in to the pressure at the base of my spine.

"Yes, Jax. Just like that." Amina hisses before her teeth latch onto my arm. Sharp incisors bite down on my bicep, as her entire body shivers from the pleasure coursing through her veins and bowing her back. I increase the tempo of my thrusts, fucking her through the orgasm and triggering my own.

When it hits, my muscles shake, forcing me to put more of my weight on her than I usually would. She releases my arm and makes a small surprised sound underneath me. For a second I worry that I'm hurting her, but then she wraps her legs back around my waist and her arms around my neck and rocks up into me, dragging her sex along my length as I spill inside her with long, hot, forceful ropes of cum that make my vision blurry.

It takes me a few seconds to come back to my senses, and when I do, Amina's trailing soft kisses from my temple down the side of my face. With so much of my weight on her, she can't reach past my cheekbone, but I relish the feel of her lips on me all the same. Before last night it'd been years since I felt her lips on me, and now I'm certain I can't ever live without them.

We stay like that for a few minutes. Heaving, sweat-slicked chests pressed together, her lips on my skin, the evidence of our relentless need for each other spilling out of her through the small space left between our joined bodies. And it's perfect. One of those moments that can't be broken by anything but the people living it. By their hopes or fears. By their failures and shortcomings. I've had a lot of time to think about mine and the role they played in losing the most important person in the world to me.

Amina sighs contentedly, and I know I have to break this moment. Because as good as it feels, it's not real. Not yet. And it won't be until we have a real discussion about where things went wrong. Right now our relationship is like a fractured bone that healed incorrectly. All jagged lines and misaligned pieces that are fused together by passion and history but don't quite fit right. If we have any hope of having anything besides these few days together, I'll have to break us again. I'll have to drag her through the end of us, make her relive the moment she lost all faith and trust in me so she can know the whole truth of it, and I know it's going to fucking hurt.

"Mina." I sigh heavily, lifting off of her, so I can see her face. Her soft, pliant expression makes me want to change course, to say something stupid to put a huge smile on her face and ignore the knot of anxiety in my chest caused by the knowledge of what I'm about to do. What *I have* to do. "Baby, I..."

My sentence is interrupted by the loud rumbling of her stomach, and we look at each other with matching surprised expressions before we burst out laughing. Neither of us has eaten anything since dinner on the yacht last night, and I know Amina well enough to know that having a serious conversation with her when she's well on her way to hangry is not smart.

Deciding to switch gears is a lot easier than it should be, and I know I'm just delaying the inevitable, but I'm desperate to hold on to the easiness between us. Even if it's just for a little while longer.

"I guess that's my reminder that we need more than orgasms to sustain us."

"You're a chef, Jax. You, of all people, should never forget about the importance of food." She cocks a sassy brow at me, and I take a little too much pleasure in seeing it fall as her expression slips into a mixture of pleasure and pain as I pull out of her. We both suck in a shaky breath, it's slow work because she's a little swollen, and the prolonged retreat feels good. *Too good.* Like I-know-we're-starved-and-exhausted-but-I-could-do-this-again, good. Amina's legs tighten around my waist, reversing all of my progress, and my gaze flies to hers.

"I have to feed you."

Her arms lift, and then she's reaching for me. And God help me, but I can't resist her. I lower myself into her hold, and she puts her hands on both sides of my face and kisses me.

"I can eat when I'm dead." She whispers between hungry slides of her lips over mine. "Right now I just want you."

My heart twists, that ball of anxiety giving way to something softer, less worried. My hips inch forward, and I'm pumping into her slowly. Her eyes are liquid fire, bursts of molten copper warming my skin and welcoming me home.

"You're sore," I tell her, still moving. Unable to stop myself, to deny her anything.

She shakes her head. "I'm fine. This is perfect."

"You're hungry." I drive into her, grinding my pelvis against her clit.

Her breath catches. She bites her lip to stifle a moan. "For you."

I take her lips again. Drinking the sound of her pleasure and pushing down those three little words that don't even begin to capture the way I feel about her. I used to think she was a blessing—a gift from God to an undeserving man—but I was wrong. She isn't a blessing, some small thing held up to prove the existence of a higher power and keep you beholden to it. She is the reason blessings exist. They are born in her eyes and fueled by the blood in her veins. They are forged in her name and written by her hand. She is my religion. Her body is my place of worship, and I will spend the rest of my life at her altar.

"Now you're the one pouring out your heart like a lovesick teenager." I pant into her mouth, surging further into her heat with my next stroke and stealing her ability to speak. Neither of us should be this desperate for each other. Not after the morning we've had, and yet the hunger is there. Impossible. Insatiable. Inescapable. And we have to feed it.

I slip my arms between her back and mattress, holding her to me while I slide in and out of her with gentle pumps that make us both feel like we're unraveling. It's not long before Amina comes, walls pulsing around me, palms running down my back, heart racing against mine. I'm not far behind her, and this time when I recover, I don't waste any time pulling out of her.

This time Amina doesn't stop me. Her limbs are boneless as they hit the mattress, and we're both breathing heavily as I lay on the bed beside her. We're still close, close enough for her to toss a leg over my hip and for me to reach out and touch her. My hand lands on her lower stomach, and I realize my mistake when she flinches at my touch. Instantly I'm hit with flashes of injecting needles full of hormones into her skin in this exact spot.

The way the tiny drops of blood would bloom and disappear with a quick swipe of my thumb. The way her skin would turn blue and purple. She would still have those marks when we went in for the embryo transfer. And then, by the time we got that second negative blood test, they'd be a pale yellowish-brown, fading away just like our hope.

73

Her hand covers mine, gentle but firm fingers wrapping around mine to push them off. Away from her skin, from her pain, from our past. I let her do it because whatever I'm feeling right now, touching the place where our child would have grown had any of our efforts bared fruit, must pale in comparison to what it feels like for me to touch her there. I chance a glance at her, and her eyes are on the ceiling, watching the wooden blades of the fan whirl around in circles.

I sit up, sliding down the bed until my mouth is level with her belly button, and place a kiss there. It's a light kiss, more of a caress, that's not about sex at all. It's about honoring her and her pain. It's about acknowledging the hurt there and promising that it won't tear us apart again. She sucks in a sharp breath as I continue laying kisses in a line that leads directly to the place my hand was just resting. When I finally make it back to my destination, that warm and perfect place just under the swell of her belly and above her cleft, I give her an open mouth kiss, sucking the skin into my mouth and gifting her with rhythmic pulls that make her squirm.

"Jax, don't." Her fingers sink into my hair and try to tug me up, but I shake her off. I don't like the way she sounds like she understands my intent to worship her and doesn't think she deserves it.

"You're perfect," I whisper, moving from the center of her body to the right and laying another kiss on a spot I remember being particularly sore after our first round of IVF. The bruises she got after the first dose of hormonal stimulants were brutal, even more so once we were told that the round wasn't successful. I remember holding her and thinking I'd never heard her cry like that before. Those soul-wrenching sobs that shook her whole body. And then, after another failed round, it became the norm. She cried every day for weeks, for months. "So fucking strong and beautiful. You're a warrior, Mina. And I'm sorry I was too busy trying to save you from the hardships of battle to appreciate how determined you were to win the war."

She covers her mouth with her hand, but I still hear the sob that breaks free from her chest. I hate myself for causing it, but I know she needs to hear these things. The unspoken truth of us. The once buried, but never forgotten, reality of our broken union. Because even though she asked for the divorce and the threads of our ending are wrapped up in Cassidy's presence in our life and my perceived betrayal, *this* is where it all started to unravel.

With high hopes sent to the heavens only to come crashing down on our heads. With the weight of the failures, she insisted on owning, pushing her further into despair and self-loathing until it was nearly impossible for her to look at herself in the mirror. And I just wanted it to stop. I just wanted her to stop tearing herself apart over something so far out of our control. She took it to mean that I wanted something different altogether. That I'd changed my mind about everything when all I'd done was decide that I wasn't prepared to sacrifice her for the sake of having children that shared our DNA.

Amina's body shakes, and I don't look up to confirm, but I know tears are leaking out of the corners of her eyes. I just keep laying kisses along her pelvic bone, over and over again, from one side to the other. Some of them short, simple caresses, some of them long, reverent, languid slides of my lips and tongue over skin that sacrificed so much for our dreams of starting a family.

"We weren't ruined, baby. And we were never over. The divorce was just our way of delaying the inevitable because we were always going to find our way back to each other. I was always going to find you and make it right."

"Stop." She gasps. "Please stop."

I do as she asks, removing my lips from her precious skin and moving up her body to kiss away her tears. Just as I thought, they're spilling down her cheeks and back into her hair, mixing with the sweat dampening the curls along her hairline.

"I'm sorry." I breathe, my own tears leaking out of my eyes. "I'm so sorry, baby."

She shakes her head, disbelief swimming in the glossiness of her eyes. "Don't."

"I know I hurt you. I know I broke us, and I'm sorry." I study her face, and the utter despair, the complete devastation, I see there makes my chest tight. "I love you, Amina." Her eyes widen a fraction, and I can see her mind spinning, trying to reconcile my words against a truth she thinks she knows. "I never stopped. You don't have to say it back right now, but I just wanted you to hear it. To know that all I've ever wanted was a life with you. Whatever that looked like. Where ever it took us."

She reaches up, cupping my jaw and rubbing her thumb over my cheek. "And now?"

"Now?"

"What do you want?"

"You, baby." I lean into her palm, relishing her touch. "Always you."

9

Amina

I'm not sure when Jax started being so fucking good with words, but I can't get a thing he said when we were in bed this morning out of my mind. His fierce tone when he called me a warrior. His soft eyes when he told me he loved me. His tortured expression when he apologized for hurting me. I thought I was going to explode when he said it, when he looked me in my eyes and all but admitted to betraying me, because hearing those words swept away the last vestiges of that old hurt. It made the part of my heart, the one that's been filling with forgiveness and hope for us since he first looked at me on the plane, overflow with love for him.

With the realization that I want him. I want his forever eyes and his broken truths. His secret smiles and his inside jokes. All of it. Everything we lost when I walked away from him. I wanted to tell him, but for some reason, I couldn't bring myself to do it. Not while he fed me fruit and waffles and eggs by hand as we sat naked in the bed. Not while we made love under the warm water from the rainfall showerhead. And not while I pushed him out of my door, so he could go back to his villa for a meeting his assistant said had to happen as soon as possible.

He wanted to take the meeting here, but I made him leave, telling him I had work I needed to tend to as well. Neither of us acknowledged the fact that it was a lie. I mean, technically I do have things I could be doing right now.

I have several emails from my own assistant sitting in my inbox—updates on contracts, schedules for upcoming shoots, a request for approval on the edits made to the video I filmed for my YouTube channel before I left, the early planning stages of a free photography workshop I want to do to teach other Black photographers how to grow their business—but the reality is, I don't want to be anywhere close to Jax's business.

Because being close to his business means being close to *her*, and listening in on his meeting means hearing her name, or worse, her voice. And I'd rather swallow a bolt of lightning than be subjected to her sultry lilt curling around every word and transporting me back to the day she used it to turn my world upside down.

Lyric forced me to go shopping for the opening. She said nothing I had in the duffel bag I've been living out of for the past few days was going to do, and she was right, so we spent the entire day trying on dresses that would make Jax forget all about the fight we had and the fact that I haven't seen or spoken to him in days. I was hoping to have an actual conversation with him, so I didn't have to hinge the entire future of my marriage on a dress and fuck-me heels, but when I went by the house last night to talk he wasn't home. So here I am, walking through the back entrance to Arcane, hoping I'll be able to catch him before people start arriving and all of his time and attention has to be on making sure things run smoothly.

The back hall, where Jax's office is located along with the break room and additional storage, is surprisingly empty, which makes me feel a little less nervous. My heels slap against the dark tile as I make my way to his door. I'm a few feet away when the door opens, and I stop, a smile already curving my lips as I prepare to see my favorite face in the world. Only it's not the familiar line of his muscular frame stepping into the hall with me. No, this is a smaller frame. Curvier. Dressed in an expensive silk blouse that's half undone and being tucked haphazardly into the waist of a pair of black slacks. It only takes me a second to realize who this person—this woman walking out of my husband's office looking like pure sex—is.

"Cassidy." I hate how my voice sounds. How small the word is, how it does nothing to reflect the shock slamming into my body with every beat of my heart.

Her head snaps up, and even though she sees me, even though she knows that I know what her appearance means, she still smiles at me as she wipes lipstick from the corner of her full lips with her thumb and arches a brow at me.

"Yes?" She starts walking towards me, long, confident strides that carry her away from the door. Away from the office where my husband must be putting himself back together again.

"What are you—" I stumble over the words, unable to decide if I want to ask a question or make a flat-out accusation. "How long?"

"I'm sorry?"

"How long?" I hiss, voice still barely above a whisper. "How long have you been fucking my husband?"

Her almond-shaped eyes laugh at me as she tucks an errant curl behind her ear, and I get the distinct feeling that she's taking pleasure in this. In standing here watching me be devastated by the betrayal of a man I've loved for my entire life.

"Amina, you should really discuss this with Jax."

"I'm discussing it with you." Because I can't face Jax, even with the betrayal so fresh in my heart, I know I won't ever be strong enough to hear him say that he went looking for attention from another woman because I was a failure. I'd failed at getting pregnant. Failed at being a good wife. Hell, I couldn't even help him make his dreams of opening a restaurant come true, but she did. She gave him everything I couldn't.

"Fine." She crosses her arms and sighs like I'm inconveniencing her. "What do you want to know?"

"How long?"

"Is that really what you want to know, Amina? Because in my experience, the main question a woman in your position really wants to have answered is 'why?' Why me? Why now? Why, why, why?" She steps closer to me, eyes dancing with triumph when I step back. Not because I'm scared, but because I don't think I can stomach smelling Jax on her skin. "You wanna know something? The answer is always the same: you dropped the ball. You took him for granted. You left him open and available for something better. And in your case, you practically gave him to me. Do you know how much you've missed while you were sitting at home shooting yourself up with hormones, crying over pregnancy tests, and wishing for a baby he doesn't even want? He built all of this—" Her arms stretch wide, indicating the building we're standing in. "—without you. And I helped him. I gave him my *money and my connections and my dedication. I've been by his side through all of it, and thank God I was because you were nowhere to be found."*

"I—" Everything hurts. Like my heart, my soul, my entire body is being destroyed. Ripped apart by the truth in her words. Jax and I haven't told anyone we're trying, let alone doing IVF. I was too scared other people knowing would add more stress to an already stressful situation, but he told Cassidy. He shared that with her.

"His star is on the rise, Amina. Jaxon Daniels is going to be a world-renowned chef by the time I'm done with him. He'll have everything he always wanted, and if you care about him, if you ever gave a single fuck about his career and happiness, you would let him out of this mess of a marriage so he can be with someone who can give him everything he wants when he wants it."

A shudder rolls through me, pulling me out of my head and away from the worse day of my life. I suck in a deep breath, pushing down the ball of emotion swelling in my chest, and forcing myself to focus on something happier. Like the moment Jax put his hands on my belly and planted kisses against my skin. Honoring my fruitless sacrifices with his lips while his words rang in my ears. I wanted to tell him that I loved him then, but fear stopped me.

Fear that we're doomed to repeat our same mistakes because the fundamental issues in our relationship, the ones that led to the affair and unraveled us, are still there. I still want kids, and I still have no reason to believe I'm able to have them naturally, which means IVF or some other form of medical intervention is the only way to make it a reality. And while time, and therapy, might have helped me deal with where that journey led us last time, I don't think I could survive it again.

You might not have to if he doesn't want kids anymore.

The internal reminder would offer some comfort if I wasn't so certain that I do. I pressed pause on my journey to motherhood when Jax and I broke up for obvious reasons, but the desire never went away. And now we're...doing whatever it is we're doing here, and I'm more in love with him than I should be but too uncertain about what our future might look like to do anything about it.

I don't know how long that uncertainty will last though, because we're not even halfway through day one, and he's already decimated all of the walls I thought I built around my heart.

"Focus, Amina," I whisper to myself, shaking off the last of my internal turmoil and opening the folder full of Lyric and Rob's wedding pictures. I uploaded them as soon as Jax left for his meeting, and it took forever for me to sort through them, deleting the repeats and images that just couldn't be saved, and now they're ready to be edited. I planned to have them done before they get back from the cruise, but that was before Jax decided to make it impossible for me to do anything but obsess over him.

With a happy sigh that would be embarrassing if anyone else was in the room, I open the first picture and start editing. I make it through about thirty photos before I break and send Lyric a few of the final edits. Within moments, her face is lighting up my phone screen. There's a slight twinge of anxiety rolling down my spine as I pick up.

"You hate them don't you?"

"What?" Lyric laughs, sounding happier than she did yesterday. "Shut up, girl. You know they're amazing. We love them!"

I breathe a sigh of relief. "Seriously?"

"Yes! Why on Earth are you acting like you don't know how fucking talented you are?"

"I'm not. I just always get worried when I deliver galleries, especially to family members."

It's true. Even now when I've shot countless weddings and hit the send button on numerous galleries, I still feel that thrum of doubt go through me while I wait for a response. And on the rare occasion that it's a family member on the receiving end of the notification email, it gets even worse.

"You did that, Mina!" Rob yells from the background, making me giggle as my nerves settle.

"Tell him I said thank you."

"I will," Lyric says. She sounds like she's walking. "He's already changed the background on his phone to a picture of the kiss. You did great, Mina. Thank you so much."

A fresh sheen of tears glosses over my eyes. "You're welcome, sis. You guys made it easy. How's the cruise?"

AGAIN

"It's incredible. We spent the night at the anchorage, and this morning we got to eat breakfast on the sundeck while we sailed through the crystal blue water. I've never felt so at peace, Mina. I wish you guys could have stayed, you would have loved it."

I laugh. "Not likely."

"Why?" I can hear the frown in her voice. "Because of Jax? I thought you guys were...better."

"No!" I yell, a little too loudly. "Not because of Jax. Because I hate boats. I always feel nauseous when I'm on them."

"What?! Rob couldn't have known that, he would have never done the ceremony on a boat if he had. I'm sorry...."

"Lyric, please don't apologize for having the most thoughtful husband in the world. You guys had a beautiful wedding, and I wouldn't have changed a thing about your day. Especially not for me."

"I mean I know, but still, you could have gotten sick." There's a slight pout to her tone, which is funny because I can tell that the thought of me not feeling well is activating all of her big sister instincts.

"But I didn't, Lyr." I pick up the glass of water in front of me and take a sip. "I'm perfectly fine."

"Just perfectly fine, huh? Has Jax's dick game fallen off since the divorce?"

I nearly choke. Water dribbles down my chin as I struggle to recover from the juxtaposition of her serious tone and inappropriate question.

"Oh my, God." Lyric is cackling now, and I picture her doubled over laughing as I wipe my chin. "Why are you like this?"

"Because I'm your big sister."

"My annoying big sister."

"Your annoying big sister who knows you got dicked down by your ex-husband last night and wants to know how it was."

"Did you really just say *dicked down*?"

She's still laughing. The sound carrying over the wind blowing against the speaker. "You're deflecting. It was that good, huh?"

I bite my lip, knowing it's pointless, but still trying to hold in my own giggle. "Better."

82

She gasps. "Mina!"

"What?! You asked."

"I know. I just don't think I was prepared for you to answer honestly." Her tone is still playful, but I can hear it turning thoughtful, serious. "Are you sure that was a good idea?"

I shake my head even though she can't see me. "No. I'm not sure about anything."

Except that I want to do it again.

"And does Jax seem sure?"

I trace the rim of my glass, picturing the man in the villa next to me. His steady calm, his resolute certainty. He's sure about everything. Sure enough for the both of us. "Yes. He wants it to be more."

"More?"

"More."

We're both quiet for a moment. All the levity from before gone. Lyric knows what Jax means to me. What we mean to each other. She watched us fall in love as kids and fuck it all up as adults. She opened her home to me when I left and held me in her arms while I cried for my husband. After a full minute, she blows out a slow breath.

"What do you want?"

My heart answers before my mouth can, and it spells out Jax's name with every beat. I close my eyes, allowing myself to feel things I've spent so long suppressing. I push up from the table and start to pace around the room. "I don't know."

"Do you really not know or are you just scared to say it out loud?" Lyric's question is gentle, but I can hear the hint of sass there. She knows I'm bullshitting. "Look, Mina, you don't have to give me an answer, but at least be honest with yourself. You wouldn't be sleeping with him if you weren't open to more."

"It's just sex, Lyric." The lie sounds lame even to my ears.

"Girl, get off my phone lying. There's no such thing as just sex between people like you and Jax. There's too much history there for it to be anything less than important."

I scrunch my nose, hating how right she is. "Ugh. Bye. I hate when you say things that make sense. Go back to your perfect honeymoon with your perfect husband."

"Guess I hit a nerve, huh?" She lets out an amused huff. "I'll go back to my honeymoon and my perfect husband. You go back to reconciling with yours."

"We're not reconciling!" I hiss into the phone, but it's too late because she's already hung up. The words settle in the silence around me, mocking me with their desperation to be truth. I throw myself onto the bed and bury my face in sheets that still smell like Jax. "We're *not* reconciling," I mumble to myself as my eyes drift closed, but the words are hollow, as empty as my life has been since I let the person who makes me happiest go.

* * *

The familiar click and shutter of a camera—not just any camera, *my camera*—wakes me. Once my eyes open, it takes me a second to realize where I am and what's happening. I roll over onto my side, neck craned and eyes searching for the source of the sound. I find it, or rather him, leaning against the dining table, long legs crossed as he holds the camera to his eye and uses steady, capable fingers to press the button and snap a photo of me.

I must look a mess right now, crushed curls, sleep in my eyes, and the print of the pillow I slid under my head before I fell asleep marring my cheek, but Jax is looking at me like I'm the most beautiful thing he's ever seen. He takes another photo of me staring at him, sprawled in the middle of the bed that smells like us and fighting the urge to reach for him, to reassure myself of my claim on him after he's been gone for hours. It was the early afternoon when I hung up the phone with Lyric, and now the sun is setting, bathing the room in golden light that reminds me of his eyes.

I sit up and stretch, enjoying the way his fingers grip the camera tighter as he captures the motion, no doubt catching the flash of the underside of my breast from underneath my crop top. "How was your meeting?"

"It was fine." He moves the camera away from his eye, so I can see his face. He looks...stressed and tired. Like whatever the pressing situation he was

84

called away to deal with took all of his energy. "I'm glad to be back here with you though."

A rush of satisfaction moves through me. "I'm glad you're back too."

His eyes flash, surprise mixing with pleasure at my honest response. "Did you have a good nap?"

"It would have been better if you were here."

He slips the camera strap over his head and pushes off of the table, crossing over to the bed. The mattress dips under his weight, and I scramble backward to make space for him. He grips one of my ankles and pulls me back down between his legs, so I'm laying back and he's straddling me. "I guess you shouldn't have sent me away then."

"Or maybe you shouldn't be taking business calls while you're on vacation." A soft smile pulls up the corner of his lips, and I watch him fiddle with the camera, adjusting the settings before bringing it back up to his eye and taking another shot of me. "When did you get so good with a camera?"

He shifts his body a little, changing angles. "A few months after you left, I was missing you. There was this emptiness in me. In my heart. In my life. And I wanted a way to feel close to you." Gentle fingers reach down, brushing a curl away from my face before tracing my brows that are furrowed in surprise. "You've been my life for nearly twenty years, Amina. Did you think that would stop just because you walked away?" I turn into his hand, nuzzling against his warm skin and breathing in his familiar scent. The camera shutters again. "So I bought a camera just like yours, it's an expensive ass camera by the way, with all the damn lenses you have, and I watched every video you ever posted online about how to use it. Sometimes I watched just to see your face and hear your voice."

My heart is pounding, trying to beat its way out of my chest. Jax's voice is so soft, so sweet while he lays out all of his truths. Truths that are setting off shock waves through my body, opening up the crack in my chest I worked so hard to patch. I hear the camera shutter again, and I wonder how the photos are turning out. If the riot of emotions happening inside of me is playing out on my face.

"You're a good teacher. I can see why so many people are pressing you to do a workshop. You have this way of making the most complicated thing seem simple, easy."

Shock ripples through me, compounding with the disbelief I feel at hearing him admit to buying a camera to feel close to me because the push for a workshop is new. Like just started a few months ago on my various social media accounts, new. I didn't realize Jax was that tuned in to what was going on with me and my business.

"You watched my videos?"

He lets out an amused huff and uses his fingers to turn my head back towards him. Our eyes lock. My heart stutters, and I fight to keep the words climbing up my throat from spilling out.

"Yes. Every single one of them, multiple times. And now I'm halfway decent with a camera."

I twist my lips to the side, letting him see that I'm not buying his fake humble act. He's clearly more than halfway decent with the camera. He holds it confidently, and when he adjusted the settings a minute ago, he didn't look at all confused by the choices that appeared on the screen. Even now, he's gone from shooting with the viewfinder to displaying the frame on the digital screen, his eyes serious as they flit between it and my face while he clicks the button to take another shot.

"You look more than halfway decent. I've seen photographers who've been shooting for decades look less confident than you do right now."

It's the truth. Some people always look like they're still actively figuring things out, even if it's something they've been doing for years. Other people, like Jax, have an easy confidence about them. One that makes them look competent, capable, no matter what they're doing. That's how he was the first time he picked up a knife after a weekend of binge-watching shows on Food Network. He was certain he could chop vegetables faster and cleaner than every chef he saw on there. By the end of that first day, he wasn't anywhere near as good as them, but he was better than me, Lyric and Rob put together.

He shrugs. "As I said, you're a good teacher."

"Did it help?"

"What?"

"Watching the videos." My chest is tight. I don't know why I'm asking. I know the emptiness he just mentioned, I live with it every day, and I know that nothing helps. "Did it help with the empty feeling?"

"No, baby." He drops the camera, finally giving me his full attention. "Nothing helped."

I reach for him, running my hands up his chest and grabbing a handful of his shirt, and yanking him down to me. His breath is warm as it skates over my skin. I lean up and offer him my lips. "Will this help?"

The last syllable is barely out before he closes the space between us and kisses me. It's a gentle kiss, a sweet claiming of my mouth that demands my instant surrender. Giving it to him is an easy decision, one that I make with my heart and not my mind. One that turns the spark of desire that's been simmering low in my belly into a flame. No, not a flame, an inferno. It swirls around me and Jax, enveloping the bed and spreading into the room. Licking at the white curtains with the same urgency that Jax is licking into my mouth.

Moaning, I release his shirt and trail my fingers up his body, slipping over his neck and face until they land in his hair. My fingernails scrape his scalp as I wrap my legs around his waist, pulling him closer. He's already hard. Heated flesh pressing into my core and making it impossible for me not to roll my hips into him. Jax groans and pulls away, moving his hips back, so our bodies are no longer fused together.

I pout at him as he removes my legs from around his waist. Then he's sitting up on the bed and pulling me with him. "What are you doing?"

"Making sure we make our reservation and giving you time to recover. I know you're sore, Amina. And as much as I love fucking you, I don't want that to be the only thing we do with our time together."

I nod, trying to hide the disappointment I'm feeling. All of it isn't because of the need swirling low in my belly. No, some of it is because I'm afraid that once we step out of this door and do something other than give in to the constant electricity sparking between us, it'll become real. Jax's forever eyes. His quiet confessions that resonate in my bones like the deepest truth. My feelings that are becoming harder and harder to push down.

"Hey." He grips my chin, pulling my attention back to him. "It's just a meal, baby. Nothing we haven't done before, right?"

Everything inside me quiets. All the worry and fear slipping away, fading into the background as I stare at the man who loves me enough to see through my fear and right into my heart.

"Right."

10

Jax

Amina's hair blows in the wind, thousands of dense strands and black coils that make up the cloud of curls on her head picked up by the salty ocean air and whipped around by the breeze until it tangles around her face and causes her to smile because no matter how hard she tries, she can't untangle it on her own. For a brief moment, I'm stuck just staring at her, soaking up her smile and wondering how we got here. Walking on the beach, wasting time until we have to be at the restaurant for our reservation. She's been holding my hand since we walked out of her villa. My heart was so full when she reached for me, when she leaned into my shoulder and looked at me like she used to before everything got so screwed up.

We laughed and talked about the most random stuff. Dancing around subjects I don't want to broach with her like past relationships because it would mean having to admit that I haven't even entertained the idea of a serious relationship since she walked away while trying to hide the fact that I know the names of every man who's so much as looked her way in the time we've been apart. There have been a few of them. Most recently some asshole named Andrew who freelances for her company sometimes. Somehow, we managed not to step on any metaphorical bombs and made it to the beach, where the setting sun and evening air love her just as much as I do.

I use our linked fingers to pull her back into me and my free hand to move the curls hiding her smile from me away from her face. She glances up at me, eyes soft and full of happiness I think I put there.

"You look happy."

Her smile widens. "I think I am."

"You think you are?" My brows fall together, and I try to search her gaze but she turns away from me to watch the waves roll in and crash at our feet. Patience has never been a strength of mine, probably because I spend most of my time in the kitchen and no one expects a chef to have any, but that's what I am as I wait for Amina's answer. Patient. Composed. Even-tempered. Because whatever answer she's formulating in her mind will be thoughtful and intentional, which means that's what I have to be as well.

After a while, she sighs and drags her gaze back to me. "I am happy, Jax, but I'm also scared to let myself be. I mean what we're doing is crazy. Three days to fix what it took us so long to break, even though nothing has changed? What are we—"

"Amina." I squeeze her hand, and she quiets. "Baby, we're not crazy, and we're not trying to fix everything in three days. This is just us beginning again. We'll have the rest of our lives to work on us, to heal what's been broken, to grow into the people we were always meant to be together. We're not going to leave here fixed, but I do hope we'll leave here committed to being the best version of us that we can be."

"How do you do that?"

"Do what?" I pull her closer to me, wrapping my arms around her waist.

"Sound so sure about everything." She pouts, actually pouts, like she's disappointed that I'm sure about her. About us. Because even though she said 'everything' I know that's what she meant. *How do you sound so sure about us?* The unspoken question breaks my heart because I know it's coming from that sad, uncertain part of her that was born on the day of the opening, created by a woman I let into our lives with information I never should have trusted her with.

And here it is again, an opportunity to do the very thing I came here to do. A chance to rebreak the bone and set us on a path to healing with nothing but truth and love between us. I should do it. I should tell her that I know what

Cassidy said to her, that I know what she made her think I did, but mentioning her name right now would feel like dealing Amina a death blow when all I want to do is kiss her.

So that's what I do instead.

I swoop down and kiss the surprise right off of her face. Taking full advantage of her parted lips and sliding my tongue into her mouth, licking into her with hungry swipes that make her moan and grab fistfuls of my shirt while she reciprocates. Her lush curves meld into the hard planes of my body, and I allow my hands to make the journey from her waist down to her ass, grabbing two generous handfuls of perfection and squeezing. We stay like that for what feels like forever, a tangled mess of lips and tongue, my hands on her ass holding her to me, her moans carried away with the breeze, and the waves crashing at our feet.

Amina breaks the kiss because I can't bring myself to pull away. And I can tell by the way she's looking at me that she's less than a second away from telling me to take her back to the room. Her pupils are blown, desire wiping out the rings of rich brown and copper, and her skin is flushed. Her cheeks and neck have a tint of red playing just underneath the surface, and I'm half tempted to take her up on her silent request, but I have to feed her before I take her to bed again.

"You're the only thing I've ever been sure of, Amina." I plant a soft kiss on her forehead, and she gives me a small hum of approval. I glance at my watch. "Now let's get some food. Our table should be ready by the time we get there."

She runs a hand down my chest and bites her lip. "Can't we just do room service instead?"

I shake my head and laugh, grabbing her hand and planting a kiss in her palm. "No. We're going to have dinner at a table, so I can make sure you take more than three bites of your food before you try to sit on my dick again."

Her nose wrinkles. "Please, you're the one who can't keep that thing under control."

I start pulling her towards the pathway that leads back to the resort. "I seem to recall you being the one pulling me back when I was trying to pull out this morning."

Just the thought of her legs wrapped around my waist, guiding me back to her slick heat, has my dick growing hard. I'd love nothing more than to carry her back to the room and rip the lightweight summer dress right off of her body, but I want to have a meal with her. One where it's just us, and I can stare at her and pretend she's agreed to be mine for more than just a few days. One where I can find something other than our physical connection to base my hopes on. Some verbal assurance would be nice.

I've been pouring my heart out to her every chance I get, but she hasn't given me a clue as to where her head is besides the brief mention of her tentative happiness on the beach. I knew this wasn't going to be easy. I knew she wasn't going to be convinced after a few orgasms and lighthearted conversations. But I did hope that by now she'd be ready to admit this feels right to her too. That she still loves me and believes that I have never stopped loving her.

Maybe then it'll be easier to tell her that I never betrayed her.

"And I don't seem to recall you protesting."

I pull her in front of me, so I can plaster my body to hers from behind, and she giggles as I nuzzle into her neck, nipping and biting at the skin there before soothing it with gentle kisses. "There's not a man in this world who would deny himself the pleasure of your body when you're offering it so willingly, Amina."

"Is that not what you're doing right now?"

"I'm not denying anything. I'm just delaying the inevitable until we've both eaten, but make no mistake, I plan on spending the rest of the night indulging in all the pleasures of your body." I kiss her neck again, and her steps falter. We stumble along the path with me licking and sucking at whatever part of her I can reach with my mouth—her neck, her shoulders, her ears—and her trying and failing to squirm out of my grasp.

When the path ends, depositing us back onto the stamped concrete bearing the Cerros logo, I release her, and she glares at me. I can tell she's trying to make it look serious, maybe even a little threatening, but all of that is eclipsed by her beauty and the barely-there smile trying to tip up the corner of her lips. Before she can get a word out, I grab her hand again, linking my fingers through hers and pulling her into my side. She settles there, still trying to look angry until I plant a kiss on the top of her head.

There are several places to eat on-site, but I decided to take Amina to Niebla—the most popular restaurant at the resort. Unlike the one we ate at with Lyric and Rob, which was in the center of the resort, this one is completely open to the beach. We follow the posted signage to the entrance, and Amina stays nestled into my side as we wait for the hostess at the booth outside the door to prepare our table, but the moment we step through the doors, starting our journey through the open-concept space, she pulls away from me. And I would be offended if I wasn't so happy about getting to see her mouth drop open and her eyes bounce from one part of the structure to the next taking in every detail. I know them, they're her photographer's eyes. The ones that capture every detail in front of them and long for the sharp, clarity of a lens to see it through, just to make sure they're getting it all.

The vast, open space that makes you feel like you've stepped into a high-end treehouse. The ringed wooden posts that lift the sinuous lines of a canopy made completely of a material that looks like wood but moves like vines to the sky. The polished cement floors with the same wood-like material inlaid, woven into the unforgiving material, following its undulating lines throughout every inch of the space. And then there's the vast, open patio with smaller, more intimate canopies over designated seating areas and a bar off to the side.

We're seated under a canopy closest to the edge of the patio, where there's nothing in front of us but the beach. Amina takes the seat across from me, still gaping at the beauty of the architecture while the hostess shows us how to order our food from the tablet on the table and pours us water from the carafe sitting between us. Then she disappears, leaving me and Amina alone. She's still studying our surroundings, and I'm still looking at her. Committing every inch of her smile to memory, admiring how beautiful she is, how the light radiating off of her makes even the most stunning backdrop pale in comparison. My chest swells with pride and the purest happiness because she's here with me.

"This place is insane!" She whisper-yells, leaning in close so I can hear her. Her eyes are vibrant and alive, glittering with excitement that lets me know the wheels in her brain are spinning. "I wish I had my camera, I could get so many amazing shots here. I have a few clients who would love it. Do you think they would rent this whole space out and transform it into a ceremony/reception space? I mean they probably would, it's a lux—" She pauses, leaning back a little and giving me a weird look. "Why are you looking at me like that?"

I don't know exactly how I'm looking at her, but I can imagine it's the kind of look that makes it evident that I'm thinking about how much I love her. How incredible and talented I think she is.

"Like what?"

She gestures vaguely towards my face, a blush creeping up in her cheeks. "Like...that! *Stop it.*"

"I'm not doing anything."

"Yes, you are. You're doing that thing with your face that you do when you're about to say something that'll either make me cry or want to drop down on my knees and suck you off because it's so sweet." I snort, and she rolls her eyes, but she's still blushing and there's a slow smile tugging at the corners of her mouth. "Don't do it. I'm not in the mood to cry, and you said I have to eat dinner at a table. I doubt they'll let us stay if I pull your dick out and make you my appetizer."

The image of her doing exactly that flashes through my mind quickly, making my dick twitch. Any opportunity to have Amina's mouth on any part of my body is always one I want to consider, even if it involves a little bit of exhibitionism, but there's no privacy here. Nowhere to bring the fantasy her filthy words have inspired to life that won't get us both arrested.

I pin her with a hard stare. "Behave."

"Why would I do that?" She arches a brow at me. "You like it when I'm bad."

"You're right," I say, taking a sip of my water to cool myself down. "But only when there's a remote possibility that I'll be able to reap the benefits of it."

She throws her head back and laughs. "And where's the fun in that?"

"In the orgasms."

"You could be having an orgasm right now if you'd taken me up on my offer

94

for room service."

Her fingers tap lightly on the table as she holds my gaze. There's so much fire there. So much need swimming just under the surface, barely contained by the sassy look she's giving me.

"And miss the look on your face when you saw this place?"

My question causes her to pull her attention away from me and take another look at where we are. After another moment of quiet observation, she looks back at me. "You're right. This is so much better than watching you come."

I roll my eyes, trying to look serious even as a huff of amusement leaves me. "Shut up."

"Wow." She places her hand on her chest. "That is unbelievably rude, Jaxon."

Her over-dramatic display has me laughing harder, which makes her smile. I fucking love her smile. "You said it first."

"Now you're resorting to transferring blame?"

"Yep." I nod, finally pulling myself together. "If you can do it, so can I."

"Oh, sweetie." She gives an exaggerated sigh, shaking her head. "Someone should have informed you that you can't do the things I do."

"If I let other people tell me what I can or can't do, I wouldn't be sitting here with you."

My tone is too serious, detracting from the levity of the moment, but I can't help it. Every conversation with my wife, no matter how it starts, will always end up like this. Colored by our history, wrought with emotion and unspoken truths.

Amina's smile slips a little as she sits back in her seat. "What do you mean?"

"Last night before we left the boat, I told Rob I was going to use our time here to see if we could work things out. He told me to leave you alone. That I couldn't change your mind in such a short amount of time."

Her shoulders stiffen. "You talked to Rob about us?"

"He's my brother, and I used to value his opinion."

"Used to?"

"Yes. Before he told me to stay away from you. Are you mad?"

She bites her lip, looking thoughtful for a moment. "No. I mean I don't think I can be because we hadn't agreed on anything then."

I breathe a sigh of relief. "Okay. I'm sorry for saying something to him before I spoke with you though. It wasn't fair for me to put it on his radar before we had a chance to discuss things."

"I appreciate that, Jax, but it's really fine." She reaches across the table, placing her hand in mine. "Besides he was going to find out anyway because I told Lyric."

All at once, my heart slows, stutters, and then stops. Time seems to freeze as I process Amina's words. It's actually quite hard to do with a brain that's recently imploded. She told Lyric. *She told Lyric.* **SHE TOLD LYRIC.** When my heart starts beating again, and my brain is reassembled, I'm able to fully appreciate what it means for Lyric to know about this. It makes it more than some emotion-fueled fling that'll be over once we leave the resort. It makes us more than a remote possibility. It makes us *real.*

Of course, we still have some things to work through, hard conversations that need to be had before we leave here, but knowing that Lyric knows makes me feel even more confident that this can work. Amina listens to her, she trusts her, and Lyric loves me, but most importantly, she knows how much I love her sister. She's seen me show up to cookouts at their place and hope by some miracle to catch a glimpse of Amina in the crowd. She's watched me turn down dates and throw myself into work because it was the only thing I could do to fill the void her sister left in my life. She knows I'll do anything to make things right, and now she knows that Amina's giving me a chance.

Which means, that for the first time since she said yes, I feel like I actually have one.

"Oh," I say, fighting to keep the excitement blooming in my chest from curling around my words. "What did she say?"

A small smirk curves her lips. "You know how much Lyric loves you, you can guess what she said."

"Yeah, but I'd rather hear it from you."

"Too bad. I won't be repeating any of her pro-Jax speeches."

"Stubborn."

She sticks her tongue out at me. "Can we order now? I'm starving, and I was promised an incredible meal, one worth missing a few orgasms for."

Before I can answer, she swipes the tablet off the table and starts scrolling through the menu, listing off items she thinks I might be interested in. I'm only half-listening though, too caught up in the hope springing in my chest and spreading out to all of my limbs to do anything but stare at her.

11

Amina

I order half the damn menu while Jax sits across from me staring like a star-struck fool. I should have never told him that Lyric knows about us because now he's going to think it means something, and I'm not sure it does.

Oh, who the hell are you kidding? Of course, it does!

That little voice inside of my head is screaming at me, has been screaming at me since Jax gave his little speech on the beach about not trying to fix everything that's broken between us in three days. His words were everything I needed to hear. They touched every worry, soothed every doubt, and pissed me off. Because they forced me to realize I'm in this. I'm *really, really* in this because committing to spending the rest of our lives working on our relationship sounds a lot more appealing than walking away when this is done.

I guess I knew I was a goner before the walk on the beach. I should have known it the minute I admitted to Lyric what I'd done because telling her was basically the equivalent to sealing my fate. And maybe that's exactly why I told her. Because I wanted to drag it all out into the light and make it known. Make it real. Make it something more than three days of 'what if' and 'maybe,' and also give me the chance to hear my sister, one of the only people I trust completely, say I'm doing the right thing.

Jax came here knowing he wanted this, wanted me. I didn't have that luxury, but I did choose this. I chose him, and I know it, but I'm scared to say it out loud because we haven't had the hard conversation yet. The one that will bring up feelings and memories that might be too painful for us to overcome, even as this new version of us.

After we finished eating, Jax and I decided to head to one of the more casual bar areas on-site for drinks and dancing. The place was packed when we got here a few hours ago, people sitting and standing all around the lit patio, laughing and drinking and dancing, but there are even more people now. It seems like the later it gets, the more people there are, which is fine because it makes Jax hold me closer as we dance. His hands are tight on my waist, his fingers digging into my skin while I grind into him, rolling my ass into an erection that's been there since we walked onto the dance floor.

We're as close as two people can reasonably be in public, but I want more. My need for him is a constant hum underneath my skin that's amplified by the alcohol in my system and the love in my heart, and I want more than anything to sate it. To feel his bare skin on mine. To feel his lips on my neck, his hands on my breasts, his dick sliding through the evidence of my need for him before easing inside me.

Jax's hands leave my waist and run up my sides, the tips of his fingers just barely graze the side of my breast, but it's enough to send me over the edge. I spin around in his hold, wrapping my arms around his neck and pulling him down until my lips are at his ear.

"I need you."

I don't give him a chance to respond, mainly because I know he'll probably make a joke about me being desperate for him and I'm not in the mood for that because I am desperate for him. Embarrassingly so. Instead, I step out of his grasp and turn on my heel, starting the tenuous process of weaving my way through the crowd of people around us with Jax at my back. He reaches forward and grabs my hand, and we navigate the crowd together with me in the lead. Once we're free, on one of the more secluded paths leading back to the villas across the resort, he spins me around and crushes me to him. I manage to get out a surprised yelp before his lips hit mine. He tastes amazing. Like tequila, salt, lime juice, and Jax, and I happily devour him. Not caring that we're out in public or that his hands are now on my ass, palming both cheeks in an obscene way that I fucking love. I arch into his touch, my hardened nipples brushing against his chest.

He groans into my mouth then pulls away. "Is that what you needed?"

"Yes." My voice is deep, husky, and a little breathless. "But also no."

I grab his hand and start pulling him down the path at a breakneck pace. And even though I'm dragging him around and contradicting myself, he just follows me. Laughing to himself and muttering something about me being a crazy woman. I shoot him a glare over my shoulder. "If I'm crazy, you made me this way. You're the one who refused to fuck me before dinner."

And now it's been hours since he's been inside me, and I feel it—that aching, empty feeling where he's supposed to be—deep in my core. The kiss only made it worse, made the hunger more acute. Just seconds ago I felt sure I could survive the walk back across the resort to the room, but now I'm not so sure. I scan the path frantically, looking for somewhere, anywhere private enough for Jax to get me off. I'm so worked up it would probably only take a few flicks of his finger to do it.

"There." Jax leans in close, plastering his front to my back like he did when we were walking back from the beach earlier tonight, and pointing up ahead. I want to ask him how he knows what I'm thinking, but I'm too busy trying to follow his finger. Eventually, I see what he's talking about. It's a structure made of the same polished concrete and wooden vines as Niebla tucked into a purposefully wild-looking arrangement of plants and trees. There's a faint light spilling out from the curved entrance, and a sign outside that says something about a tranquility garden, but I don't get to read it fully because we're moving so fast. Jax guides me towards it with his hands on my waist and his lips at my neck. When we get closer, I can see it's a partially enclosed alcove with a small bench inside and a surprisingly peaceful, and well-lit, water feature on one wall. As soon as we step inside, Jax lets me go.

"Sit down." I do as he says, because apparently being horny means my instincts override my common sense, and sit on the bench. It's hard and a little uncomfortable, but discomfort is to be expected when you're about to do whatever it is we are about to do in public. Jax stands over me, his eyes doing a quick sweep over me, and then to my shock, and complete pleasure, he drops to his knees in front of me. "Tell me where you need me, baby."

His voice is a raspy caress that swirls around me, brushing against my skin and landing right between my legs where my clit is throbbing, demanding his attention. My heart is in my throat, and the air is thick between us. Laced with need, brimming with desire that's his and mine and ours. Jax looks ready to jump on me, and I kind of want him to, but he hasn't moved a muscle. Every inch of him is still, awaiting my instruction, and I know he'll stay like that until I tell him what I need from him. How I need him.

I spread my legs, and the second my thighs part, Jax's lips follow suit. He watches me as I take the hem of my dress between my fingers and pull it up until it's bunched at my hips. I have to hold the fabric in one hand, but with the other, I reach down and move my panties to the side. They're soaked through, so they stick to my bare sex just a bit. Jax sucks in a sharp breath, his body rigid, still waiting for me to give him a direction.

"Here," I whisper, eyes locked on his as my fingertip grazes my clit. "I want your mouth right here."

In any other situation, a man as tall and muscular as Jax would look awkward shuffling around a concrete floor on his knees, but when he does it, closing the small space between us, it just looks sexy. Like he's kneeling at an altar preparing to commit a sin he'll have to repent for later. When he reaches me, he runs his fingertips up my legs, tracing a path from my ankles to the apex of my thighs where he moves my hand out of the way. Then he's leaning forward, placing his nose right at my core and breathing in deeply. I shiver as his breath rushes over my heated skin.

"Here?" He murmurs against my skin, his lips ghosting over my clit and making my hips jerk forward.

"*Yes.*"

"Lean back, baby."

My head collides with the cool concrete of the wall behind me as Jax sits up and wraps his fingers around the fabric of my panties. I feel the lace digging into my skin, but the sensation is brief, passing quickly as the sound of the lace ripping fills the air. Lightning rolls down my spine and all of my breath leaves me in a whoosh as I watch Jax toss the ruined scrap over his shoulder. He flashes me a devilish smile as he slides his fingers between the backs of my thighs and concrete, lifting my legs and pulling me down to the edge of the bench, so I can rest my legs on his shoulders.

I open my mouth to beg him to get on with it already, but the words melt into a moan as he licks me. His tongue flat and hot as it glides through my folds, starting at my center and ending at my clit, which he takes into his mouth. He gives me the barest graze of his teeth over the bundle of nerves before hollowing his cheeks and sucking rhythmically on it. My back arches and my hands come up, fingers sinking into his scalp and pushing him further into me. I rock my hips, biting my lip to keep the desperate pants crawling up my throat from coming out and drawing attention to what's happening here. Anyone could be on the path right outside. Anyone could walk in here and find Jax on his knees, holding me up to his mouth and making distinctly satisfied noises in the back of his throat that make it sound like I'm the most exquisite meal he's ever had.

"Ohh, Jax." My grip tightens, and I'm probably hurting him, but I don't care. All I care about is the pressure building in my core. The sweat beading on my brow, and Jax's mouth. His mouth that's hot and incessant and working at me with the kind of single-minded determination any woman in my position would appreciate. "*It's so good.*"

He hums his assent, sending pleasure vibrating through me. My walls clench, searching for something to bear down on, and I wish that his hands weren't occupied, that he could sink two of his fingers into me and fill the emptiness there. Balancing my weight on one hand, Jax pulls my fingers from his hair and guides it down to my sex. I don't even think to question what he's doing, I just trust him to know what I need and give it to me. And when he releases my clit with a rough growl, replacing his mouth with my hand, I know that he deserves my confidence.

"Rub your clit and keep your eyes on me, Amina." He rasps, kissing his way down to my entrance. "I want you to watch me while I fuck you with my tongue."

He puts his hand back under me, tipping me up further so that my aching sex is level with his mouth. I stare up the length of my body, eyes riveted to the sight of his wicked tongue transforming into a spear I know he's going to use to destroy me. *And God, do I want to be destroyed.* My index and middle finger run down both sides of my clit, while the others hold my lips open, giving Jax an immaculate view of the pussy he's about to fuck. Pleasure courses through me when his eyes flash with heat as he rims my entrance with his tongue. Circling it three times before he finally dips inside, lapping up the moisture spilling out of me with every shallow thrust. It's not as satisfying as the sensation of having his dick filling me, but it's exactly what I need right now. My back bows and I cry out, rolling my hips to meet his thrusts while my fingers rub my clit in furious circles that have pleasure searing my veins. I'm panting desperately, moaning his name and not giving a damn about who might hear me because I'm chasing the ecstasy tightening every muscle in my body and blurring my vision.

He knows that I'm getting close, and he holds me tighter to his mouth. His tongue plunges in and out of me over and over again, making it nearly impossible for me to keep my fingers where I need them to be. It doesn't really matter though. Because within seconds of him doubling his efforts, I'm coming apart around him. My entire body shaking violently as my thighs clench around his ears, forcing him to stay where he is while I'm washed away by a tidal wave of pleasure that's like nothing I've ever felt before. And he doesn't seem to mind being held hostage at all because I feel him pull out of my quivering walls and start to lick at me—my lips, my clit, my mound—with gentle strokes of his tongue that draw out my orgasm or induce another one altogether. I'm not entirely sure. I just know that by the time I come down, I'm boneless, sated, and unbelievably tired.

Jax slides my legs from his shoulder slowly, placing my feet on the ground one by one and then righting my dress. Before he rises to his feet, he picks up the scrap of fabric that used to be my panties and tucks it into his pocket. I try to sit up, to move, to do something other than recline back on this bench like a rag doll, but I can't.

"Come here, beautiful." His words are coated with pure, masculine pride, and I roll my eyes but take the hand he's extended to me. I let him pull me up and into his chest, enveloping me in a bone-crushing hug. I breathe in his scent and burrow further into him. I want to be closer. To feel like there's nothing between us except for a layer of sweat-slick skin. Jax drops a kiss to the top of my head before letting me go just enough to lean back and look at me. "Let's head back to the room."

I nod lazily and let him lead me out of the alcove by the hand. We keep our fingers linked as we walk the winding paths back towards the beachside villas. The moon is high in the sky, and there are hardly any people around, which makes me feel less awkward about walking around with no panties on and the evidence of my orgasm slicking my thighs. Soon we're standing outside of the villa, and Jax is digging the key card out of his pocket and opening the door. He gestures for me to go ahead of him, and I step through the door, kicking my shoes off at the entrance and pulling my dress over my head.

I'm reaching back to unhook my bra, when Jax comes up behind me, moving my fingers out of the way and doing it himself. When the last hook is loose, he snakes his hands around to my front, large palms covering the cups and holding them up so I can pull my arms through the straps.

"So gentle with the bra after you demolished the matching panties," I mutter, shaking my head.

He laughs softly before dipping his head to press a kiss on my shoulder. "They were in my way."

He's running his hands down my body, over the sides of my breasts, down my rib cage, and back up again. It's a mesmerizing, incredibly relaxing, cycle that has my head falling back to rest on his shoulder.

"You could have just removed them."

"And make you wait another second after you said you needed me? Not fucking likely."

Slight outrage coats his words as if he's personally affronted by the idea of me having to wait for anything, especially pleasure. Especially from him. That does something to me. Something that makes me care even less about my ripped panties and ruined matching set. Something that makes me spin around in his arms and stand up on my tip-toes to claim his mouth in a kiss that's sweeter and more emotion-filled than any we've shared thus far.

Jax responds to me immediately, slanting his lips over mine and taking over the kiss. I can taste myself on his tongue, and it makes me wild for him. I run my hands under his shirt and begin to push the fabric up his torso. He breaks the kiss for a second, reaching back behind him to yank the shirt over his head with one hand while the other keeps me anchored to him. When his lips crash back into mine, we're both a lot less gentle, and the tender kiss dissolves into a frantic clashing of lips and teeth and tongue until it feels like we're both trying to eat each other alive.

And I love every second of it, all of the fatigue I felt from my earlier orgasm is gone. Replaced by a need that's pulsing in both of our veins, replacing our blood with liquid fire. I wrap both of my arms around Jax, and he plants both of his hands on my ass, lifting me up and carrying me to the bed. He lowers me down to the mattress with the kind of gentle awareness I wouldn't expect him to have right now.

Once I'm settled, he pulls back again, and I let out a frustrated groan that only lasts for a second once I realize he's unbuttoning his pants and shoving them down his waist to free his dick. Then he's covering me again, his bare chest pressed to mine while he reaches between us to guide his length to my core. I'm already wet and ready for him, so he doesn't waste any time teasing me when he finally gets the tip aligned with my entrance. I watch his abs flex as he swings his hips back and then thrusts into me, sheathing himself in my heat. Stretching me out with the thick, veined perfection of his shaft. Possessing me in a single stroke that has me coming in an instant.

"Oh, God!"

The orgasm catches me completely off guard, and Jax fucks me through it. Pushing into my spasming walls and angling his hips so the flared tip of his dick hits my g-spot repeatedly. It's a relentless, luxuriously torturous pounding of his flesh against mine that pulls the most obscene, beautifully broken sounds from me as one orgasm rolls into another and another. A never-ending cycle of pleasure and ecstasy that I can't quell because Jax won't stop pumping into me, using his body to drive pleasure into mine. He holds me in place while I writhe underneath him, screaming my pleasure at the top of my lungs.

By the time it stops, I'm a whimpering, spent mess, and he's panting above me. Sweat beading along his hairline, the veins in his neck bulging, the muscles in his forearm straining underneath his skin, and his face is the picture of concentration while he chases his own release. His brows are furrowed together, a little dip that I want to kiss sitting between them while his eyes stay glued to mine. His pupils are blown. Rings of gold washed away by a decadent, smoky black that burns right through me. Right through the last vestiges of my resistance, and leaving nothing but the raw truth I'm not sure I can hold inside me any longer.

I close my eyes and concentrate on the feeling of Jax moving inside of me, meeting his every thrust with a roll of my hips that's only meant to aid him in finding his release. After that onslaught of pleasure, I know I can't come again, but it still feels good to have his dick dragging along the sensitive tissue, teasing me with the possibility.

"Look at me." The dark gravel of his baritone forces my eyes open, and I'm thankful for the order because otherwise, I would have missed this. The moment his smooth strokes turn jerky. The moment every line in his handsome face contorts, transforming into a mask of gratification as he finally allows himself to let go. Flooding me with scorching hot cum that mixes with the moisture from my orgasms and leaks out of me and onto the bed.

Jax rests his forehead on mine. His chest heaving. "You feel so fucking good, Amina. *We* feel so good together. Don't ask me to go back to a life without this, without you, I won't do it. I can't."

"Jax—" My voice is barely a whisper, but he hears me, hears the hesitance in my voice, all wrapped up in one syllable, and he lifts up just a little to look at me.

"I know, baby. I know you're scared. And I promise I'm not asking you for an answer right now. I just want you to know how I feel. I don't ever want you to have to wonder about whether I really want this because I do. It's all I want."

* * *

The next morning Jax wakes me up with soft kisses and a gentle order to get my ass out of bed, so we can go out sightseeing. When I mumbled my protest and told him to leave me where I was, he slapped my ass, dragged me out from underneath the sheets, and carried me into the bathroom where he already had the shower running. After we brushed our teeth and washed our faces, he ushered me into the shower where I stood just outside the spray of the warm water to avoid getting my hair wet again.

Jax took it upon himself to get us both clean. He started with me, pouring my favorite body wash onto a washcloth and lathering it up. I half expected him to use it as an opportunity to do more than cleanse my skin in smooth, but efficient, circles, but he never did. And when he was done with me, he told me to get dressed, make sure I put on a bathing suit, and not to climb back into bed.

Resisting that order was no small feat because I was tired, worn out from the emotional and physical aspects of our reunion, and very much looking forward to a day of not having to leave the bed. Somehow, I managed to get my clothes on and slap my hair into a mess of a bun by the time he got out of the shower, and I'm glad I did because getting to see Tulum—the real, vibrant city—outside of the resort is an incredible thing.

There's so much to see here, so much culture, so much beauty. We've been out all day, and I still don't feel like I've seen half of it. Our morning started with a tour of the Mayan ruins and then we took a bus down to the actual jungle, where Jax listened to me stress about bugs and snakes while we hiked to a cave I wasn't sure I wanted to see. He promised me it would be worth it, and he was right. Because it wasn't just your regular everyday cave, it was a cenote, and we got to spend the afternoon swimming in bluish-green water surrounded by limestone and hanging vines that he made me swing from more than once, just so he could get multiple pictures of me trying to cannonball into the water.

It was the most fun I'd had in a long time.

Our late afternoon was a lot less adventure-packed than our morning. When we left the cenote, we got lunch in the city then spent a few hours walking around the markets, buying souvenirs and acting like the cheesy tourists we are. After the market, I was ready to go back to the resort and pass out, but Jax said he had one more thing he wanted to show me, so now we're in the back of a van on the road that leads to the resort while he rubs my feet and refuses to tell me what our last stop is.

"Just tell me!" I wiggle my toes at him, and he rolls his eyes.

"We'll be there in two minutes, then you can see for yourself."

"Jaxxxx," I whine. "I've seen enough. Just describe it to me, I've got a very good imagination, you know."

"This from the woman who told me not to put brussel sprouts on the menu at Arcane because she couldn't *imagine* anyone wanting to put them in their mouth."

"Brussel sprouts are disgusting, Jax. No amount of bacon is going to change that."

His laughter fills the small space we're sharing, wrapping around me like a warm blanket. I bask in the feel of it, in the knowledge that I might not have to go back to a life without it.

"They're our most popular side," he says, digging his phone, which has been ringing an awful lot today, out of his pocket and frowning at it before sending it to voicemail. I avert my gaze, forcing myself not to ask if it's about work, if it's Cassidy on the other end of the line trying to get his attention.

You can't run from this conversation forever.

I know I can't, and I don't intend to because I know there's no way Jax and I can have a future if we don't hash out every part of our past, and that includes her. It includes him owning his betrayal and me deciding whether I can live with him still being in business with her after what happened.

"Well, I guess no one who eats at your restaurant has good taste."

"Guess not." He sticks his tongue out at me and slides my shoe back onto my foot as the van begins to slow down. It makes a turn that looks like it's taking us towards a beach, except there are signs for hotels and other things I don't get to catch as the van goes further down. Eventually, we come to a stop, and Jax hops out, extending his hand to me and helping me out of the van.

"Where are we going?"

"Just a little way down the road," he says, taking my hand and heading down the winding path bathed in golden sunlight. "We have to walk it though."

"Okay." I agree, not like I have much of a choice since he's already pulling me behind him. I take in our surroundings, noticing small groups of people who look like they only come to places like Tulum to take pictures for their feed coming from where we're headed. After a while, we turn down another path, this one lined with trees that make it feel like we're back in the jungle. I'm just about to ask him how much further we have to walk when I see it.

Well, not it, *her.*

A huge sculpture made of wood and rope and metal, towering above us. It's a woman, and she's beautiful but sad with a wooden crown on her head and intricate carvings in her sullen face and arms. But it's her hands that stop me in my tracks because they look like they're ripping her apart. Carved fingertips breaking through layered wood, holding it open to expose the lush greenery in the middle, leaving a cavern in her center big enough for a person to walk through.

"She reminds me of you." Jax's voice is hushed, nearly silent, and the heat from his gaze warms my face. I can't meet it though, I'm too riveted by what's in front of me, by his suggestion that *I* could bear any resemblance to something this beautiful.

I give him a puzzled look. "Forgive me if I don't see the resemblance."

"I'm not talking about looks. Do you see how her hands are positioned? How it looks like she's tearing herself apart for the sake of others. For the people who want to pass through her. For the plants that want to thrive inside her." He slides a finger under my chin, turning my attention to him. *"That's* where I see the resemblance. Because you did that for us. Every time you pushed a needle into your skin. Every time you wore the bruises like battle scars. Every time you picked up the shattered pieces of both of our hearts and got ready to try again. I watched you tear yourself apart, Mina, trying to make our dream of having a family a reality."

My heart sinks into my stomach, and all the muscles in my body tense as I prepare for the moment where he tells me that my obsession with getting pregnant is why things went the way they did.

"And I was scared for you," he continues, the words catching me completely off guard. "I didn't want to watch you go through that over and over again. I didn't want to bear witness to you destroying yourself for something I would have been happy to have with you regardless of how we got it. The day I told you I didn't want to do the last round of IVF, that's what I should have said. I should have made it clear that I wanted you and every single bit of the life we planned to have together, but I wasn't willing to lose you to get it. I wasn't willing to watch you wreck yourself to give it to me."

Tears shine in his eyes, making the rings of gold and quartz turn glossy. I can see the faintest bit of my reflection there. The shock and confusion etched into my features. The love shining in my eyes. The sadness sweeping through me and making my lips tremble as I wonder how the man standing in front of me, *saying these things*, can be the same one who betrayed me.

"It wasn't just your dream, Jax." I reach up and wipe a tear from his eye. "It was mine too, and neither one of us could have expected it to be..." *Detrimental. The beginning of the end.* "...so hard. We did the best we could, and it wasn't good enough then, but I hope this time will be different."

"It will be." He holds his arms open, and I step inside, letting him envelop me in the warmest, safest hug. One that makes me feel like I can survive anything as long as he's by my side.

12

Jax

After our exchange in front of the wooden woman sculpture, Amina gave me a long, meaningful hug. It was one of those hugs full of meaning, one that said a million things without saying anything at all. Then, as soon as we started walking back to the van, she disappeared inside her head. We rode back to the resort in silence, and that's what I've been sitting in—save for the sound of the shower running in the bathroom—since we got back to the villa.

I'm okay with the silence, though, because it gives me to time deal with the non-stop calls I've been getting from Cassidy today—handled with a curt text message that told her to direct all of her calls to my lawyer—and think of a way to bring up the final, most painful, part of our divorce. A part I didn't know about until three weeks ago when I was making the rounds on the floor at Arcane and came across Cassidy at a table with her friends talking about Amina showing up to the opening and staying for less than fifteen minutes.

To say I was confused by what I'd overheard would be an understatement. A huge fucking understatement, because up until that moment, I believed with everything in me that my wife hadn't shown up to the opening. I believed that she'd finally had enough of IVF, of the stress and pain, of her absent husband who spent more time with his investor and her friends than he did at home. I believed it, and although it hurt me, I accepted it. And when the divorce papers came, I signed them.

I set her free.

I thought I was doing the right thing, the honorable thing, giving her a chance to find something different, something better, but I didn't know that to Amina, my decision not to fight for her was just confirmation of my wrongdoing. And how could I have known? No one around us breathed a word about my alleged infidelity. No one so much as suggested that my wife was leaving because I cheated on her. *Not even Amina.*

So years went by. Years she spent being haunted by images of an affair that never took place. Years I spent only half-understanding why I was living without her and maintaining a friendship with the one person in my life who knew.

It only took me a minute to pull the truth out of Cassidy. Once I got her away from the table, it all came out. Her twisted logic and the ugly lies she told my wife in some backward attempt to get me to see her as something other than a friend. My mom raised me not to hit women, and not doing so had never been a challenge for me, but that day it was. I wanted to tear Cassidy apart limb by limb, to hurt her the way she hurt Amina.

By some small miracle, I managed to walk away without laying a finger on her, and by the time I got home from the restaurant that night, I'd formulated a plan to get her out of my life for good. A plan that started with buying her out of Arcane, the only one of my restaurants I needed her money to start, and ended with never speaking to her again.

Amina doesn't know about my plan to buy her out. She doesn't know that once we leave Tulum, when we go back home and figure out how our new life looks together, she'll never have to worry about Cassidy. If I have my way, she won't ever see her, hear from her, or be lied to by her again.

The water in the bathroom shuts off, and I set my phone on the table in front of me, shifting my body in the chair, so I'm facing the door when Amina comes out. I pull in a deep breath, ready to lay out this last bit of truth, so we can finally have all of our cards on the table.

When she emerges, she's wrapped in a big, fluffy white robe that makes me want to hug her. To take her in my arms and kiss her like it's the last time I'll have the chance to because for all I know it might be. There's a reason I've been running from this conversation, why I've been avoiding doing what I know needs to be done: I'm scared she won't believe me.

I'm scared she'll hear my words and still choose to hold on to the lie she's carried in her heart for so many years. It's had a chance to settle in her bones, to embed itself in her brain, to override every single good memory that used to live there, and I know some people would think it doesn't matter because even with that lie in her heart she's found a way to give herself to me, but it fucking matters to me. I want to destroy that lie. I want to untangle it from the fabric of her being. I want to shred it with my words and watch how it heals her heart.

"What's wrong?" She's standing in front of the closet, flipping through the dresses hanging there. I study the line of her jaw while she plucks a simple shift dress off a hanger and throws it on the bed, completely unbothered by my silence and staring. My phone buzzes on the table, drawing her attention back to me. I decline the call, and she lifts a brow. "Are you okay?"

"Yeah, I just need to talk to you about something, and I'm not sure how to do it."

I watch her face, wondering if she'll take in my grave tone and flat expression and realize what it means. If she'll know immediately that I want to talk about the day she decided to leave me. It only takes a second for it to hit her, understanding etched into her solemn features. She takes a seat on the edge of the bed and rolls her shoulders back, steeling herself, like she's preparing for me to break her heart instead of put it back together.

"Just say it."

"A few weeks ago, I found out you came to the opening. You never told me that you showed up."

"I—" She presses her lips together like she's trying to think of the right words. "We weren't exactly on speaking terms at that point. Or afterward. How did you...who told you I was there?"

"I overheard Cassidy talking about it with some of her friends."

"Oh."

"She never told me about seeing you that night."

113

"Really?" Her eyes flash, a lethal mix of hurt and anger aimed at me. "I'm surprised she didn't manage to fit it in between your celebratory rounds of fucking in her high rise."

The certainty in her words, the absolute fucking belief she has in their correctness, sets something loose in my chest. I should have been prepared for this. I knew she believed Cassidy, believed her enough to walk away without so much as confronting me, enough to divorce me and never tell me the real reason why, but hearing her say it, hearing the way the lie has calcified, hardened until it became a twisted truth, hurts like hell.

My hands curl into fists, and I feel my knuckles pop. "That would have been pretty hard to do considering how I spent the night after the opening in our home. Alone."

She blows out a long breath. "What's the point of this conversation, Jax? Do you want me to give you a pat on the back for not sleeping with her after the opening? I guess I could, except your restraint isn't really that impressive when I know for a fact that you fucked her beforehand."

"I never fucked her, Amina." A loud buzzing fills the room, nearly drowning out my words, and my phone screen lights up with another incoming call. I stab the decline button, not bothering to see who's blowing me up. "I never touched her. I never cheated on you."

"You don't have to lie, Jax. I saw her leaving your office. Her shirt was half undone. Her lipstick was all smeared and her hair was a mess. She looked like she'd just....she was leaving *your* office."

"And I wasn't in there. I was in the kitchen, helping the team prep. The only time I went in the office that night was an hour after dinner started to change into a suit, so I could walk the floor."

"Then who was she in there with?"

This was the part I had the most trouble getting out of Cassidy. She didn't want to tell me. She wanted to keep the focus on us, on what she'd done to get me all to herself. Admitting that she was fucking another guy in my office minutes before she took a sledgehammer to my marriage didn't exactly help her get the point across.

"Some hedge fund manager she brought as a date."

Both of her brows pinch together, and I see the emotions dancing in her eyes shifting. Anger and hurt giving way to horror. A single tear slips down her cheek. "But she said…"

"She lied, Amina, and you believed her."

"What was I supposed to think, Jax?"

"You weren't supposed to think anything!" My voice shakes as my own anger and hurt surface, fracturing my calm. I didn't want it to go like this, but having this conversation right now, looking at Amina while she tells me that she had no faith in me, it hurts. *It fucking hurts.* "You were supposed to *know* that I love you. That I would never do anything to hurt you. That I would die before I betrayed you."

"But you did betray me!" She screams, launching herself off of the bed. She's all fire and pure rage as she paces in front of me. "Maybe you didn't sleep with her, and maybe I shouldn't have believed it all so easily, but I was in pain, Jax. I was hurting, and she saw that, and she used things she knew about me—*things you told her*—to drive the knife deeper. You shared everything with her. You told her about us trying when no one, not even Lyric, knew."

"I know. I know, baby, and I'm so sorry. I fucked up, and I'll own that until the end of my days, but you could have given me a chance to explain. You could have talked to me before you closed the door on eight years of marriage without a second thought."

Amina pauses, turns towards me slowly, and I feel like I'm in the path of a hurricane. Most people would run, but I want this. I want all of her fury, all of her pain because the only way out of this mess we've made is through the storm.

"Without a second thought." She snarls. "You think I didn't think about it, Jax? Do you think I didn't agonize over the images your friend planted in my head with knowledge that you gave her? You think it didn't kill me to believe you could betray me like that and still love you more than I loved myself?"

"Amina—"

"NO!" Her chest heaves, and her voice shakes. "I gave you an out. I gave you a chance at a future, a life where you could be happy. Where you could be free of the heartbreak of being with someone who would never be happy with not having the one thing they always wanted. I kept your baggage, absolved you of your vows. I. Set. You. Free. I made you available for the future you were so eager to chase, the one I was holding you back from."

I feel it leave me. The last ounce of calm, the last vestige of self-control. Amina's words leech it from my body, pulling it from my pores and depositing it into the air. And her beautiful fucking face, crumpled and tear-stained, swallows it whole, sucking it into a black hole where I can't reach it.

"I NEVER WANTED A FUTURE WITHOUT YOU!" I scrub both of my hands down my face. Hating myself for raising my voice and growling in frustration when my phone starts to ring again. "Jesus, fucking, Christ!"

"Just answer it." Amina sighs. "I'm sure it's *important.*"

The emphasis she puts on the word important tells me exactly where her brain is right now. In our living room on the day we were in the middle of the fight about IVF and I answered Cassidy's call because I couldn't take another second of Amina looking at me like I'd ripped all of the goodness out of her life.

"No. This is important. Everything else can wait."

The phone stops ringing, the vibrations from it buzzing on the wooden table finally fade away, and then it starts again. Amina scoffs and flicks her eyes between me and the phone, looking like she might launch it at my head if I don't answer it.

"We can't talk with it ringing off the hook, Jax."

"Then I'll turn it off..."

"So you can spend the rest of this conversation wondering if one of your restaurants is burning down? I think not. Answer the damn phone, Jaxon!"

I hate this. I hate having my attention pulled away from her when we're in the middle of the most important conversation of our lives. And I hate that she expects me to, that she believes whatever is happening with my business is more important than her.

When have you given her a reason not to?

I close my eyes, the buzzing of the phone on the wood pounding into my skull. I hear Amina moving towards me, and then I smell her—that clean, perfect mix of lavender and vanilla so close I can taste it. She stops right beside me, reaching over me to grab the phone off the table. Then I feel the cool metal and glass against my heated skin and hear Grayson's disembodied voice spilling through the speaker. She's talking a mile a minute, frantically spitting words at me that I can't grasp on to, let alone comprehend.

"Slow down, *please*."

"You need to come home. ***Now.*** I've booked you on a flight back that leaves in an hour."

13

Amina

Two of the most important moments in my relationship with Jax have ended the same way: with a phone call and a slamming door. The only difference between this time and the last is that he's the one who left. That and the fact that I was the one who made him answer the phone. Oh, and the kiss. The gentle peck on my lips as he listened to Grayson—not Cassidy—fire off information into his ear at rapid speed. It must have been important, whatever she was saying, but he still took the time to kiss me and tell me that he loved me and would call me once he got this situation sorted, so we could finish our conversation.

That was two days ago, though, and outside of a text he sent to let me know he landed safely, I haven't heard from him.

Now it's Friday, the day before Lyric and Rob's big celebration, and I miss his stupid face. I miss his voice, his touch, his smile. I miss the way his arms feel wrapped around my waist. I miss the way his eyes touch every part of my face before they move to any other part of my body. I miss the way his lips feel pressed against mine, and I miss the life we had together before I let the words of a woman I never trusted ruin us.

When Jax told me about Cassidy's lie, relief flooded me. I felt peace settle over me like a blanket. Peace that had been gone from me since the second I watched her step out of his office. And even though I wanted so badly to not

118

be the foolish, untrusting woman who couldn't see past her own pain to the truth, I believed him. The moment the words hit the air, I knew they were true, and it made me angry. It made me sad. It made me want to build a fucking time machine and set everything back to rights.

Except I can't do that.

I can't take back my lack of faith or get us back the years that it cost us. I can't undo the pain it caused both of us. I can't make any of it right, and I didn't realize until after he was gone that he never asked me to. He was angry and hurt that I didn't trust him, but he never once demanded that I apologize for it because he understood where it came from. He understood *me*. The way he always has.

"It's all going to be okay, Mina," Lyric says, leaning into the mirror to fix her lipstick. "He'll come back, and you guys will talk, and it will all be fine."

My sister is some kind of saint. We've just finished rehearsing for her wedding, and instead of going over details for the real thing with the event coordinator, she's back in my villa with me, making sure I'm okay. She's been like this since she and Rob returned from the yacht. She took one look at me and forced me to tell her everything about what happened between me and Jax. When I got to the part about the opening, she told me that I was an idiot for believing that Jax would ever cheat on me. I might have burst into tears at that part, which softened her towards me a little, and she's been handling me with kid gloves ever since.

She's even gone out of her way to keep our parents, specifically my mom and Jax's mom, off of my back since they arrived yesterday. If it wasn't for her, I would be fielding questions about Jax non-stop, and that's not something I can handle right now.

I set my camera bag on the table and try not to think about the first night Jax and I spent together here. "I hope you're right."

"I am." She smiles and turns around to face me. "Now come on, I don't want to be late for the rehearsal dinner."

"Go ahead without me. I need to back the photos I took up and send off a few emails."

Her smile turns rueful. "You mean check your phone in case Jax called."

"Maybe."

"Well, at least you're being honest with yourself." She laughs, moving towards the door. "Don't be too long, okay?"

"I won't."

She gives me a quick wave and then she's out the door. I sit down at the table and begin the short work of backing up the pictures to my hard drive. Once that's done, I pull out my phone and do something I haven't done in years: check Jax's social media. I don't know what I expect to find there—some kind of indication that he's still in Fairview or on his way to Tulum, a clue as to why he had to leave so quickly—but it's not there. Exiting out of the apps, I open up the message he sent me, wondering whether or not it'd be worth it to text him. I don't know if he'll respond. I don't know what I'll say if he does. I don't know how I'll feel if he doesn't.

With a sigh, I toss my phone on the table. Everything in the room is quiet except for the sound of the ceiling fan turning in lazy circles, my breathing, and an electronic whirring it takes me too long to realize is coming from the door. I jump out of my seat, eyes searching the room frantically for something to use in case the person coming through the door isn't a member of the hotel staff. I come up empty, which is fine because as soon as the door swings open, I catch sight of a familiar set of broad shoulders. Of rich, brown skin that I dreamed about last night. Of surprisingly sexy curls I've gotten used to sinking my fingers into way too quickly.

"Jax."

He steps inside the villa, letting the door close behind him, and he looks good but also incredibly tired. Like he's just fought a long battle that he might not have won. I don't even let him take another step into the room before I start walking towards him. It takes me less than a second to close the space between us, but he sees me coming, and he drops his bags and opens his arms. I launch myself at him, standing on my tip-toes and wrapping my arms around his neck, raining kisses along every part of his face I can reach. When I land on his lips, he takes my face in both of his hands and holds me there.

He tastes like home.

Tears flood my eyes and fall down my cheeks as I try my damnedest to eat him alive. To devour him, to take so much of him into me that there is no difference between his being and mine. It feels like he's trying to do the same thing, and my heart sings its assent. My body begs me to let him.

When we pull away, we're both breathless. Smiling like fools and covered in my tears. He wipes them away with gentle brushes of his thumbs over my cheeks.

"Hello, beautiful."

"I missed you," I murmur.

Both of his brows fall together, knit with clear confusion. "You're not mad at me for leaving?"

I think about that for a second, searching for the right way to say that I don't care that he left because I'm too glad he's back. I'm not sure I can be angry with him anyway, not when I answered the phone and put it to his ear, making a decision for him, for both of us. Obviously, I didn't know it was a serious work situation, but I knew it could have been.

"No, I'm not mad at you."

"It's okay if you are, Mina. I left in the middle of another important conversation..."

"Technically," I cut in, running my hands down his chest. "I left the last time, and that wasn't fair of me. I should have stayed and talked through it with you. But this isn't the same situation at all."

As the words leave my mouth, washing over Jax and soothing the wrinkles in his forehead, I realize that they're true. This isn't the same situation. We're not the same people we were all those years ago. Somehow, someway, we're stronger and maybe a little better for the time we've spent apart.

Jax doesn't look convinced. "Are you sure? Because I'm happy to pick up where we left off."

"No need." I wrap my arms around him again and bury my face in his chest. "I heard everything I needed to hear and said everything I needed to say."

"So you believe me?"

The question comes out in a rush, making my heart squeeze just a bit for him. I pull away from his chest, craning my head back to look at his face. He looks worried and a little sad like he thought I wouldn't accept his truth. And I guess that's my fault because I didn't before.

"Yes." I nod slowly, searching his eyes, letting my heart shine through mine. "I believe you, and I'm sorry—"

His mouth crashes into mine, cutting me off. My apology gets lost in the desperate glide of his lips over mine, and when he pulls back I don't even remember what I was going to say. Jax gives me another soft peck. "I forgive you."

"Just like that?"

He nods. "Just like that. I know how we got there, how we ended up so vulnerable. It won't ever happen again."

I think back to his words on the beach, to his hope that we can spend the rest of our lives repairing what was broken between us, and I realize that he was right. These few days together didn't fix everything, there's no way they could have, but they're a start. A foundation to build the rest of our lives on.

"No," I whisper, pressing my forehead to his. "It won't. Now, tell me why you didn't call. I was worried."

He releases me, trading his hold on my waist for a grip on my hand as he leads me over to the bed. We both take a seat on the edge, our bodies turned towards each other.

"I know. I'm sorry for worrying you. I just..." He shakes his head, pulling in a breath. "There was a lot of shit I had to deal with in order to get back here in time for the wedding."

"What kind of stuff?"

The vein in his temple starts to jump, and my heart drops. It must be something bad. "What is it, Jax? What happened?"

"I'm going to tell you everything, but I just need you to be prepared because it does involve Cassidy and that night."

"Okay," I say slowly, wondering what exactly a lie from years ago has to do with the work emergency that required his immediate attention and presence.

He pulls my hand into his lap, lacing our fingers together. "When I found out what Cassidy did, I was pissed. I couldn't believe I had been so stupid. I let her into our lives, and she hurt you. She hurt us. And I knew I couldn't have someone like that in my life anymore. I cut her off immediately, but I knew not dealing with her personally wouldn't mean shit if I was still in business with her."

Understanding trickles through me. I know exactly where this is going. "You brought her out."

"That was the plan." His eyes search mine. I don't know what he hopes to see there. "We sent over the proposal before I got on the plane, before I saw you. It was a good deal, more than any of my other investors would get, I thought she would take it and be done."

"But she didn't." *Of course not.*

"No, she didn't."

"So she rejected the deal, that isn't exactly a reason for Grayson to send up a flare and demand your immediate return."

"Right." Jax laughs bitterly. "It's not, but her calling my other investors and trying to buy up their shares to give her controlling interest in the restaurant is."

"*What?*" There were two other investors for Arcane, both with fifteen percent ownership in the restaurant compared to Cassidy's twenty percent. The other fifty percent was Jax's, making sure he had controlling interest in his brainchild. But if she managed to get both investors to sell their shares to her, that would make them equal. "Why would she want to have equal ownership? It's not like it could stop the buyout."

"But it would give her more room to negotiate terms. To drive up the cost of buying her out by thirty percent or more."

I squeeze his fingers, imagining the amount of stress he's been under in the last few days. It's no wonder he didn't call. If someone was trying to take The Collective from me, I would be putting all of my time, energy, and attention into stopping it from happening.

"So what did you do?"

He takes his free hand and cups my jaw. "I beat her to the punch. I split my shares between my other two investors, giving them equal interest."

If he wasn't holding it up, my jaw would be on the floor right now. "You did *what*?! You sold your shares in your very first restaurant? You gave it all up for her? Jax, why would you—"

"I didn't give it up for her, baby." His voice is whisper-soft, but it hits me like a punch to the gut. "I gave it up for you, and I got paid very well to do it."

"But I just..." I'm stumbling over my words, unable to fully comprehend what he's saying. "I don't understand. All of that work. All of those years spent building your business, your brand, around the success of that restaurant. Just gone in an instant. Nothing is worth that, Jax."

"*You* are." His thumb brushes over my bottom lip. "Your peace of mind is worth it. The life we're going to build together—one free of reminders from a painful past full of mistakes—is worth it. There was a time when I put that place before you, where I made you feel like achieving my dreams was more important than having you, and I'm not going to make that mistake again."

My heart pounds. Fresh tears spring in my eyes. A bubble of tangled emotions swells in my chest and explodes, turning into a happy sob that bursts out of me. "You have me, Jax. You didn't have to sell your restaurant!"

"Yes, I did," he murmurs. "You had your heart broken in that place, Amina, so badly that you left me. And at first, I thought it would be enough to just be rid of her, but I realized on the flight back home that it wasn't. If we're going to do this—*and we are going to do this because I am never letting you go again*—we need to be free from all of it."

A tear slides down my cheek, following the tracks of the ones that fell when we kissed just moments ago, and Jax leans down to kiss it away. His lips caress my cheek, laving over skin that must taste like salt and joy.

"I love you." I sigh, the confession coming easily. Every muscle in his body goes still for a second, then he explodes into movement. Pushing me back on the bed and anchoring himself on top of me. His forearms are on either side of my head, his legs on either side of my hips, and his eyes...his eyes are pure fire, and I see the word forever dancing in the flames.

"Say it again."

14

Epilogue

Jaxon

M y wife is the most beautiful woman I've ever seen. Looking at her, sharing space with her, breathing her air, it never gets old. There are days when I come home and see her sitting on the couch, or working in her studio, and wonder how on Earth I got lucky enough to win her heart twice in one lifetime. Then I remember that fortune favors the bold, and when I won it the second time—almost a year ago to the day—I was nothing if not bold. I was relentless, tireless, dogged in my pursuit of her smile, of her laugh, of her forever, and there isn't a person in the world who can look at my life now and tell me it wasn't worth it.

Especially on a day like today, when I'm standing in a hospital room, watching her sleep while I hold our daughter in my arms. I thought Amina was a warrior before, but after today I have to come up with a whole new word to describe her, to capture her fierce screams and her bone-crushing grip on my hand, to reflect the pure strength of her pushes and her unyielding determination to ensure that our girl—Maya—was healthy and perfect before she even let the doctors and nurses touch her.

I've never seen her more beautiful, and I've never loved her more.

I feel like I've said that a million times since we came back from Tulum—when we brought a new house and she let me spread her out on the island and make her pussy the first meal I consumed in our new home, when she dropped the positive pregnancy test on the nightstand beside me a couple of weeks later, letting me know our efforts to christen our home had made our dreams of having a family a reality—but each time, it's been the truth.

The little bundle of perfection in my arms stirs, drawing my attention away from Amina and back to her. I stare down at her face and am once again hit with that familiar rush of serotonin, of love in its rawest form. She's just a pale little thing, with a scrunched-up face, balled-up fingers, and a head full of black curls that she got from Amina, but she's everything I've ever wanted out of this life. Everything I've ever needed, and nothing that I deserve.

"Stop being a baby hog," Amina whispers. I lift my eyes from our daughter's face and see that my wife already has her arms out, the rings I gave her when she became Mrs. Daniels again glittering under the soft fluorescent light as she reaches for Maya. "Give her to me, I need baby snuggles."

"You need to rest," I whisper back, but I'm already moving towards the bed, unable to deny the woman who's just given me the best gift I've ever received anything.

She looks like she's going to say something smart, but the moment she feels the weight of Maya's body in her arms, her entire face transforms into a soft smile. "God, she's so damn perfect."

I lean over the side of the bed, pressing a kiss to her forehead. "Just like her mama."

The End

About the Author

J.L. Seegars is a dedicated smut peddler and lifelong nerd who's always had a love of words, storytelling and drama. When she isn't writing messy and emotionally complex characters like the ones she grew up around, she's watching reality TV, supporting her fellow authors by devouring their work or spending time with her husband and son.

Also by Janil Seegars

Restore Me: The New Haven Series– Book #1

Restore Me is an enemies to lovers romance about forbidden romance and love after loss. It is the first book in the New Haven Series—an interconnected, series of stand-alone novels.

Printed in Great Britain
by Amazon

84293258R00081